SPECIAL ELECTION

BROCK CLARKE

SPECIAL ELECTION

ACRE
CINCINNATI 2025

Acre Books is made possible by the support of the Robert and Adele Schiff Foundation and the Department of English at the University of Cincinnati.

Printed in the United States of America

Designed by Barbara Neely Bourgoyne
Cover illustration based on a photograph of Lawrence Welk

ISBN-13 (pbk): 978-1-946724-92-2
ISBN-13 (ebook): 978-1-946724-93-9

The press is based at the University of Cincinnati, Department of English and Comparative Literature, McMicken Hall, Room 248, PO Box 210069, Cincinnati, OH, 45221–0069.
www.acre-books.com

Acre Books titles may be purchased at a discount for educational use. For information please email business@acre-books.com.

In memory of Rupert FitzAllan Chisholm III:

a great name for a great man

Our plans were so beautifully laid out, ready to be carried to action, but with magnificent certainty God laid them aside and said, "You have forgotten—mine?"

—FLANNERY O'CONNOR

CONTENTS

SPECIAL ELECTION

SPECIAL ELECTION

Heaven

Is there a heaven? No. There are, instead, many heavens, each of them populated exclusively by people from your state or province or canton or . . . well, Lawrence Welk doesn't know all the names for "states" in the many places of the world. All he knows is that he was born in North Dakota in 1903, and when he died in 1992 and went to heaven, it was filled with other people from North Dakota. Now, he's alive again, and back in North Dakota, the real North Dakota, and he's sitting in the office of the chairman of the state's Democratic Party.

Special Election

The chairman explains the situation. There had been an election, for the governor of North Dakota. The Republican who was elected has died. He didn't die after taking office; he died before taking office. He didn't die after being elected but before taking office; he died before he was elected.

"The voters elected a dead man!" Lawrence Welk says. This seems incredible. He wants to know how such a thing could happen. He wants to know how he got here. He wants to know how you can go to sleep in heaven and then wake up on earth. He wants to know what year it is. He wants to know about his children, whether they're still alive, whether they're well, whether he can see them. He wants to know why the office doesn't have wood paneling. Every important man's office should be paneled with wood, Lawrence Welk thinks.

"Yes, they elected a dead man."

"Did they know he was dead?"

"Well, some of them must have."

"And now you want them to elect me!" Lawrence Welk says. "A man who was dead but now is alive!"

The chairman nods. He says, in a bored way, as though reciting from a manual, "If the voters elect a candidate who has already died and gone to heaven, then heaven must send two people back from heaven to run for that office." The chairman then leans back in his chair and hooks his hands behind his head. He is a small man with a large gut and an open suit jacket and a long tie. "It's a special election," the chairman says.

Party Line

"But I'm a Republican," Lawrence Welk says.

"The Republicans already chose their candidate," the chairman says.

"Who?" Lawrence Welk asks.

"Not you," the chairman says.

Checking In

Lawrence Welk says first he must check in with his wife, Fern, who also was born in North Dakota, and who died three years after Lawrence Welk. Fern is back in their heaven. He communicates with her silently, with his eyes closed, as though in prayer.

There she is, in a field. Her right hand is encased in leather. Perched on it is a goshawk. In heaven, Fern has taken up falconry.

"I won't go if you don't want me to go," Lawrence Welk says, and at the sound of his voice the bird's eyes become huge. In them, Lawrence Welk sees chaos, he sees distrust, he sees will, he sees appetite, he sees the bird seeing the mouse parts that Fern will feed the bird if the bird flies away, and then comes back, when Fern tells it to.

"Won't go?" Fern says softly, her eyes on the bird's eyes. "Lawrence, you're already gone."

Reunion

"And my children?" Lawrence Welk asks the chairman. "Are they still alive?"

"Yes."

"Wunnerful! When can I see them?"

"When it's time," the chairman says.

"When will it be time?"

"When you've won," the chairman says.

Late Bloomer

A knock on the door and in walks a man who is obviously the son of the chairman of North Dakota's Democratic Party. They look identical except that the son has lived some decades fewer and is wearing a zipped-up fleece vest, not a suit jacket, over his too-long tie. The tie dangles out of the bottom of the vest in an unseemly way. The son's name is Ryan, although he assures Lawrence Welk that Lawrence Welk can call him Ry. Lawrence Welk notices that Ry's father raises his right eyebrow when Ry says, "You can call me Ry." Lawrence Welk has always been a good noticer. For instance, when the father says, "Ry is your campaign manager," Lawrence Welk notices that Ry's father says it like even he doesn't really believe it's true.

Then, Ry and his father have this conversation, right in front of Lawrence Welk.

"So who's he?"

"He's Lawrence Welk."

"But who *is* Lawrence Welk?"

"A famous big band leader who had his own TV show."

"From back in the day?"

"Back in what day?"

"Back in the day when big band leaders were famous and had their own TV shows?"

"No. He became famous only after all the really famous big band leaders stopped being famous. That's what he was famous for."

Homework

Ry points at Lawrence Welk—who, for reasons that are not clear, not even to Lawrence Welk, is grinning—and asks, "But why him?"

"Figure it out," Ry's father says. He hands Ry a book. On the cover, a photo of a grinning Lawrence Welk. And over his head, the words *Wunnerful, Wunnerful! The Autobiography of Lawrence Welk.*

Growing Up

Lawrence Welk was born in a sod house. The sod house was built by his father, who, before he built the sod house Lawrence Welk was born in, had built another, somewhat smaller sod house.

Lawrence Welk was raised on a farm, but he couldn't milk the cows, or kill the chickens, or butcher the hogs. Or, he could, but he didn't want to.

"I don't understand how you can mess up simple jobs!" said Lawrence Welk's father to Lawrence Welk.

"Dummer Esel! Can't you do anything right?" said Lawrence Welk's mother to Lawrence Welk.

When a neighbor offered Lawrence Welk a piece of candy, he took the whole bag.

Lawrence Welk stopped going to school when he was eleven because, it was agreed, he had learned enough math.

Lawrence Welk's first language was German. It was also, for a long time, his only language.

"That little house in back" is what Lawrence Welk called the family outhouse.

"Das kleine Haus hinton" is what he actually must have called it.

Setting Up

A feed store parking lot in Killdeer. In the lot a stage, hastily assembled, draped with red, white, and blue bunting. The buzzing microphone. Ry, fiddling with the amplifier. Lawrence Welk is wearing a red and black checked suit with a red, light blue, dark blue, green, and orange striped shirt. His tie has the same stripes, but the stripes are wider, and slant in a different direction than the stripes on the shirt. The suit is fifty years old, and it still fits him perfectly.

Just a Number

One hundred and seventeen years old.

Is how old Lawrence Welk is.

If you include the years when he was dead in the calculation of how old he is.

One hundred and seventeen years old.

Is also how old Fern is, using the same method of calculation.

Best Self

In heaven, Lawrence Welk learned that one has a best self, and at whatever age one became one's best self in life, one will be that age in heaven, for eternity.

Lawrence Welk became his best self at age sixty-seven.

Fern at age twenty-eight.

Crowd Control

Standing in the parking lot, eleven people. Few enough to count. All white men. Men in large boots and lined sweatshirts and baseball hats. Men standing with their feet wide apart. Men with their big arms crossed over their big chests. They are all wearing wide belts and attached to those belts are holsters and in those holsters are phones. One of them removes his phone from its holster and holds it up, face high. Nowadays the phone, Lawrence Welk has been told, is also a camera. Lawrence Welk looks directly at this camera phone. This was something he learned the first time he was alive: Look directly to the camera, as though there is a human being on the other side of it, because there is.

Who Are You?

Ry waves Lawrence Welk over to the edge of the stage, and they have this conversation, whispering, away from the mic.

"You know who these guys are, right?" Ry asks, gesturing toward the crowd.

"They're farmers."

"They're not farmers," Ry says.

"Of course they are!" Lawrence Welk says. After all, his father was a farmer. He grew up around them. He recognizes their sleep-creased faces. Their chapped hands. Their slow, methodical meatiness. Their distrust of new things. A man come back from the dead is a new thing. But then, it's also an old one.

"They used to be farmers," Ry says. "But they're not anymore."

"What are they now?"

"Nothing."

Failure. It is the thing that keeps us apart. The shame of it. But Lawrence Welk thinks it should be the thing that brings us together. It is the only thing we all have in common.

Lawrence Welk walks to the front of the stage. "Gentlemens, I understand how you feel!" Lawrence Welk says into the microphone, and then he tells the story of the time his band quit on him, and Lawrence Welk got undressed and went back to bed. *In the daytime.*

First Night/Worst Night

Two of the men shrug and head into the feed store. A few of them scuff the pavement with their boots. The man holding up his camera returns it to his holster and squints up at the sky, as though checking it for signs of rain. Lawrence Welk can feel the embarrassment in the air. It is theirs, but it is not his. He knows better. This is his first campaign stop. Thirty-five stops in twelve days. The first night is always the worst night. This was another thing he learned the first time he was alive.

God

There is one reporter in the feed store parking lot. She wants to know if Lawrence Welk has met God in heaven.

"Of course!"

"What's he like?"

"He's wunnerful!"

God

Lawrence Welk has in fact never met God, but on his first night in heaven God left him a note on his pillow that read, "We will not meet, so that you will continue to believe in Me."

Checking In

"I miss you," Lawrence Welk says, but Fern doesn't answer. She's having trouble with her goshawk, who is pecking and tugging at the leather glove, but lazily, as though it's just another minor annoyance. "I don't understand why you're doing this," Fern says, to the bird, but Lawrence Welk answers anyway.

"I think I can do some good," Lawrence Welk says. "And I want folks to know me again."

Squeezebox

Lawrence Welk's earliest memory was crawling across the floor of their kitchen toward his father, who was playing the accordion.

Lawrence Welk's father had inherited the accordion from *his* father. Lawrence Welk's father had had it in Odessa, and then when he emigrated he brought it on the ship with him to New York, and then on the train with him to North Dakota.

Like his father, Lawrence Welk had double-jointed fingers, and double-jointed thumbs.

In order to save up for and buy his first accordion, Lawrence Welk trapped and killed squirrels, for which he received two cents a tail.

Lawrence Welk paid fifteen dollars for his first accordion, and it broke. He paid twenty dollars for his second accordion, and it also broke.

His third accordion cost four hundred dollars. His father paid for it, and in exchange, Lawrence Welk was his father's indentured servant for four years. The accordion eventually broke, too, but not for a long time. On it, in block letters made out of rhinestones, was the name LAWRENCE WELK.

Music Appreciation

Lawrence Welk stands in the bed of a pickup truck outside the Walgreens in Watford City. Ry is standing next to him, holding what Ry calls a "portable speaker." But aren't most speakers portable? Out of that speaker, music, singing. "Who is this?" Lawrence Welk asks. Ry tells him: "Toby Keith." The sound is tinny. The music is trash. Lawrence Welk distrusts men with two first names. "Very nice-ah," he tells Ry. When Lawrence Welk hears music, he will always say it is "very nice-ah," even if it isn't.

Reverie

This crowd is even smaller than the first. Five pharmacists on their break. Drinking coffee and smoking cigarettes and looking at their phones. They are not looking at Lawrence Welk through their phones. They are looking at their phones as a way not to look at Lawrence Welk. Lawrence Welk knows from his days as an accordionist, a bandleader, a TV personality, that you don't wait for someone to look at you before you perform; you perform so that someone will look at you. "I'm so glad you're here-ah," he says, because it's true, because it's always true: No matter how few of them there are, he's glad they're here. That's part of his job: to say he's glad. The other part of his job is to make them as glad as he is. But before he can say more there's a gust of wind and the pharmacists' smocks lift and flutter and Lawrence Welk remembers a summer night at the fairgrounds in Ellendale. A rainstorm had canceled a baseball game across the grounds and had sent the players scurrying for cover under the pavilion tent. The flapping of the canvas in the wind. The stomping of the dancers on the floorboards. The quick hands of the ticket takers. The cheerful relentlessness of the polka. The baseball players and their wet hats, their soaked-through uniforms. The string lights glittering in the darkness.

Rule #1

"Rule #1," Ry says. They are in their room at the Motel 6. One of the pharmacists, it turned out, took a picture of Lawrence Welk during his reverie. The pharmacist did not send, or give, the photo to Ry. The pharmacist did not even inform Ry that he was taking the picture, that the picture even existed. But there the picture is anyway, on Ry's phone. The world is remarkable, Lawrence Welk thinks. "Don't smile like that," Ry says.

"Smile like what?" Lawrence Welk asks. Ry taps the phone. Lawrence Welk looks and there he is, smiling. It is how he has always smiled. Teeth visible, top and bottom touching lightly. The ends of the mouth go up, up, up.

"Like that." Ry taps the phone again. "Don't do that. It looks insincere."

"It does?"

"Yes," Ry says. "It looks too much like a smile."

Rule #2

"And what's rule #2?" Lawrence Welk asks, and Ry looks startled.

"Wait, did my dad tell you there's a rule #2?" he wants to know.

Checking In

In life, Fern spent most of her time in the house. In heaven, she spends most of her time outdoors. Now, she is cross-country skiing. Skate skiing, she tells him. Not classic.

"I'm weak on policy, but strong on personality." This is what Ry has told Lawrence Welk, and this is what Lawrence Welk tells Fern. But it's not clear that she hears him over the clacking of her skis, the loud, even rhythm of her breathing. Fern is sheathed in Lycra. Canary-yellow. One-piece. Lawrence Welk knows, later, he will dream about Fern in that bodysuit. Surely it is not wrong to dream about your wife, in that way. Then why does it seem wrong? That is a rhetorical question. His wife is now thirty-nine years younger than he is. It is like he is ogling a younger man's wife. On Fern's shoulder is the goshawk. It is looking backward, at Lawrence Welk. Fern is looking forward, toward a hill. A considerable hill. Lawrence Welk does not ski, but even if he did, he knows he would not be able to ski up it. He could make it on foot, probably, if there were a bench to sit on halfway up.

Fern is now climbing the hill. As she does, she cuts a vigorous series of v-shapes in the snow with her skis. It is her first time skate skiing and already Fern has mastered the herringbone.

You Asked

Ry outside the motel room, talking to his father on the phone. The walls are thin and Ry's voice is loud.

"When have I ever let you down?" Ry asks, and then Lawrence Welk listens for a long time to Ry listening for a long time.

Name Game

Ry walks back into the room and hands Lawrence Welk the phone. "He wants to talk to you," Ry says.

"He was born Sebastian Ryan Liddon," Ry's father says to Lawrence Welk. There are no phones in heaven, and Lawrence Welk has forgotten that feeling of someone suddenly in your ear. "We called him Sebastian. Because that was his name. But then he wanted to be called Seb. So we called him that, for a time. After that, it was Lid. Sebby. Ryan. Sebastian again. Liddy. S.R. Twenty-Six, because in eleventh grade that was his football number. Veintiseis, because he was taking Spanish. Shoe, because one of his friends thought he was nutty. Like a cashew. Bumblebee. His wife called them that. I have no idea why. Now they're divorced. He's forty-four years old. Now, he's Ry, I guess." Then Ry's father says goodbye and hangs up.

Moving Out

When Lawrence Welk had satisfied the terms of his indentured servitude, and asked if he had his father's blessing to go out and try to make his living as a musician, his father said, "No."

When Lawrence Welk said he was going to do it anyway, his father said, "Well, you'll be back. You'll be back just as soon as you get hungry. You'll be back in six weeks."

Although this same man would later walk back and forth outside where Lawrence Welk's band was playing and say to strangers, "Hear that music? That's my son, the leader of the band."

In order to get men who didn't dance to come to his dances, Lawrence Welk would, before the dance, teach them how to dance.

Lawrence Welk played weddings, for days in a row. At the end his left wrist was ravaged and bleeding from the accordion's leather strap. He would tie a clean white handkerchief on the wrist and keep playing. And when he bled through that handkerchief, he would put on another one.

The first time Lawrence Welk played a dance after midnight he was afraid that that would be enough to send him to hell.

Platform

Lawrence Welk's first press conference. Breakout Room 1B in the Holiday Inn in Bismarck. Ry reminds Lawrence Welk to keep it simple. Taxes, Ry says. Immigration, Ry says. Guns, Ry says. Ry says that there are two kinds of North Dakotans: those who think things were better in the past and the thought makes them happy, and those who think things were better in the past and the thought makes them want to punch someone in the face. Just tell them which kind of North Dakotan you are, Ry says. But Lawrence Welk doesn't think that he's been brought back to life just so he can say the things that Ry says he should say. Besides, he's neither of those kinds of North Dakotan.

Lawrence Welk walks to the podium. The reporters are sitting in folding chairs. Half the chairs are empty. The reporters hold their phones high in the air, in salute. Lawrence Welk suddenly feels martial. He would love to walk out of this breakout room and find a parade somewhere. "The time you are living in is the best time!" Lawrence Welk says to the reporters. And then, to clarify, he adds, "The time you are living in is always the best time."

Polling

Do you watch the Lawrence Welk Show on North Dakota PBS?

Yes: 8%

No: 75%

Who? 17%

An Effective Communicator

In the America's Best Inn in Bismarck, Ry and Lawrence Welk on their twin beds, shoes off, watching Lawrence Welk's opponent's press conference on television. Lawrence Welk's opponent wears a suit and a baseball hat. The suit is a business suit but it fits the man like a wetsuit. So many visible muscles and bulges. Lawrence Welk wonders if his opponent knows that the purpose of clothes is to conceal what is underneath them. When a reporter asks what the opponent considers a hostile question, the opponent turns around his baseball hat so he can get as close as he can to the reporter's face so he can scream into it.

Cause Of

Lawrence Welk asks Ry if his opponent has also been brought back from heaven, and Ry says he has. Ry says the opponent died while trying to disarm an IED.

"A what?"

"An IED. An improvised explosive device."

Lawrence Welk thinks about this. Words are wonderful. But there is a finite supply of them. You should use as few as possible, in case you really need the other ones later on. "Do you mean a 'bomb?'" he asks, and Ry shrugs and says, "Sure." "So he was a soldier?" Lawrence Welk asks, and Ry says no, he was a civilian, a civilian who in his garage just liked to make, and then unmake, improvised explosive devices.

Choice

Ry wonders how Lawrence Welk has never met the opponent in heaven. But in heaven, unlike in life, you don't have to meet anyone you don't want to. You can spend eternity alone, if that's what you want to do.

Checking In

Fern is sitting on the deck, on a folding camp chair, legs crossed, a tall can of beer in the chair's beverage hole. The goshawk is inside the house, in its cage, with its hood on. When Lawrence Welk asks why the bird is being punished, Fern says that the bird is not being punished. No, she and the bird are just having a little conversation.

Roommates

Lawrence Welk does not mind having a roommate, in theory. Lawrence Welk has always had roommates. There were of course his siblings, and also Fern, and their children, and his bands, the Hotsy Totsy Boys and the Honolulu Fruit Gum Orchestra and of course the Champagne Music Makers, and they had always roomed together on the road—in motels and hotels and campground cabins and in the rooms under the eaves in the seasonal resorts of the north and also, he's not too proud to say, in buses and his first Chevrolet and many times on cots and in sleeping bags in the fields of farmers. Lawrence Welk has always liked farmers, and they have always liked him. Every farmer in the world is my friend, Lawrence Welk has always liked to say.

But now there's Ry, who is high. Ry assures Lawrence Welk that he doesn't do "the needle drugs," nor the opiates, the pharmaceuticals—the "real life-wreckers," as Ry calls them. But Ry does enjoy marijuana—he enjoys talking about it, and he enjoys consuming it, in all its forms: in the form of a cigarette joint, and in the form of a liquid from an eye dropper, but especially in the form of candy that Ry calls a "gummy." In Lawrence Welk's opinion a grown man should not say a word like "gummy," at least not as often as Ry says it. "You want a gummy," Ry keeps saying to Lawrence Welk. It is not in the form of a question. Ry seems to assume that Lawrence Welk would of course want a "gummy." Lawrence Welk likes to think of himself as a good roommate, but Ry's feet smell and also, no, he doesn't want a "gummy."

Curriculum Vitae

Ry has passed out, with his laptop computer open, and on the laptop his resume.

Waiter. Pet Wash Associate. Waiter. Vitamin Entrepreneur. Waiter. Home Health Aid. Waiter. Substitute Teacher. Waiter. CEO and Founder of Our Crème Brule Is AOK. Waiter. Waiter. Self-Employed. Campaign Manager.

Silent Prayer

"Lord, let my new life be like my old. Let it have purpose. Let it be happy. Let it not be wasted."

Redundancy

"But Dad, it's an added bonus," Ry says in his sleep.

Of Age

Lawrence Welk's first band after he left home was a children's band. The Jazzy Junior Five. Lawrence Welk's bandmates were eleven years old. Lawrence Welk himself was twenty-one years old.

Lawrence Welk was also twenty-one years old when he discovered that there was such a thing as a divorce.

Lawrence Welk was also twenty-one years old when he learned to speak English.

Lawrence Welk was twenty-four years old when he had his first drink. He never developed a drinking problem. But the person he had his first drink with did.

Language Barrier

In the breakroom at the chicken processing plant in Cavalier. Lawrence Welk stands at one end of the room, next to the microwave. On the other end of the room is the whirring soda machine, and two dozen brown people wearing hairnets and red-stained white gowns. Lawrence Welk knows what his opponent has said about these people. Lawrence Welk knows what Ry has said about them. "Ninety-nine-point-nine percent of them aren't even registered to vote," Ry told Lawrence Welk before he walked into the plant, but Lawrence Welk doesn't believe that's an official tally. The manager's white face fills the window in the breakroom door. He's told Lawrence Welk that Lawrence Welk has five minutes. Lawrence Welk clears his throat and suddenly, there it is, the ghost of the baton in his right hand. He tells the workers about the immigrant farmers he'd grown up with, the immigrant farmer his father was, the Germans, the Swedes and Norwegians and Russians. "They couldn't speak English, but they were the most American Americans I've ever known."

The workers don't say anything. One of them, a women, turns and plugs some coins into the machine, and a can rattles and thunks its way down the chute and into the bin. The woman removes it, cracks it open with the same hand that's holding the can. Lawrence Welk wonders if she too has double-jointed fingers and thumbs. Lawrence Welk would like to get an accordion in her hands and see what she could do with it. Lawrence Welk would like to get him in her hands and see what she could do with him. Where did that thought come from? Begone! Lawrence Welk says, to his thought. Begone is a word he didn't know he knew until he thought it to say it to his thought. The woman takes a drink and Lawrence Welk swears he can see the soda gurgle down her throat. Not all of it. A splash ends up on her chin, and she wipes her chin with her hand, and then wipes her hand on her gown.

"We can speak English," the woman says. She has missed his point. How difficult it is to communicate one's meaning, Lawrence Welk thinks. He will try again. He is ready to try again. But already, the manager is knocking on the door.

So You Say

Lawrence Welk can't pronounce the letter "d."

Likewise, he can't make the "th" sound.

"Telethon" he pronounces "telatawn."

"Wonderful" sounds like "wunnerful."

"Ah." Being the sound Lawrence Welk sometimes adds to the end of words. He can't help it. Or he can, but he doesn't want to.

"Lady and gentlemens," Lawrence Welk said at the beginning of a speech he didn't want to give.

"The Shampoo Music Makers" was what Lawrence Welk once called his band, the Champagne Music Makers.

He has been known to say "microscope" when he's meant to say "microphone."

"Pants" when he meant to be saying "pins."

"Coundry" not "country." "Music-ah" not "music."

Lawrence Welk was good at taking old sayings and making new sayings out of them.

About something he did not like, he would say that it was not his cup of dish.

And he was always afraid of painting himself into a condition.

"You know how bad I talk!" was another thing Lawrence Welk liked to say.

First Debate

"He talks like a retard," Lawrence Welk's opponent says about Lawrence Welk, during their first debate. Then, he turns his baseball hat around in anticipation of Lawrence Welk saying something about it. When Lawrence Welk doesn't, when Lawrence Welk just stands there, smiling at his opponent, his opponent mimics the retarded way that Lawrence Welk speaks. The impersonation is meant to be cruel, and it is cruel. It's also spot on. Lawrence Welk applauds. "Very nice-ah!" Lawrence Welk says.

Poll

Please finish this sentence: The more Lawrence Welk is verbally abused by his opponent without fighting back,

The more I feel bad for him: 31%

The more I want him to get what's coming to him, that dope, because he deserves it: 49%

The more I don't know what to feel about him: 20%

Checking In

"How do you think I did in the debate?" Lawrence Welk asks. He's afraid of Fern's answer. Fern has always been honest. This has always been what it means to be Fern, or to be married to Fern.

But Fern says she didn't watch the debate. It was at the same time as her writing group's weekly meeting. Today, they were workshopping her think piece: "The World Is Seriously Fucked, and That's OK."

Almost Verbatim

"The world is seriously fucked" is something Lawrence Welk's opponent also said, during their debate, although he did not seem to think it was OK.

Fore

December 1927, when the snowbanks were so high you had to tip your head back to see the sky. December 1932, when Lawrence Welk and his band played an outdoor show in Elroy, wearing overcoats and knitted caps, because it was thirty-seven below and that's cold! December 1941, when the weather was so unbearable that Lawrence Welk and his band decided to pack up and head south, to South Dakota.

This December. Lawrence Welk and the president of the state chamber of commerce, playing the nine-hole municipal course in Hurdsfield. The grass is still somewhat green. It is shirtsleeve weather. The sand trap is unraked. Maybe the world *is* seriously fucked, Lawrence Welk thinks, even though, up until now, to be Lawrence Welk was to think it definitely was not. His Titleist skitters over the green and into the rough. Lawrence Welk has never thrown or snapped a golf club before, but he is tempted. He pictures his opponent's neck, with the wedge wrapped around it. He pictures his wife and her goshawk. They are headed somewhere, he doesn't know where, except that it's away. But suddenly, honking from above. "Look!" he tells the chamber of commerce, who is also in the rough and pretending not to be improving his lie. Lawrence Welk points his club skyward at the geese, the miracle of their flying V.

Lessons

In a secondhand store in Rugby, Ry has bought a record player, and some records. In his lap, *Yessongs*; on the cover an image of a towering rock formation. The record is not inside the cover. It's lying on the floor somewhere, in a pile of other uncovered records. This is something Lawrence Welk must teach Ry. You must take better care of your music. There is a pile of marijuana on the album cover. That is what Ry is teaching Lawrence Welk. How to separate the buds from the stems, the seeds, the shake.

Enough About Me

Ry, high, again, talks about his wife. Why she left him. There is nothing unusual about it, Lawrence Welk thinks. Ry's wife left him for reasons people leave other people. The only thing unusual about it, to Ry, is that it happened to Ry.

It is like taking a drug, listening to other people tell their sad stories. Lawrence Welk feels high, or at least how he imagines it feels to feel high. He closes his eyes, and when he opens them, Ry is staring at him. Time has passed, but how much of it?

"You were about to tell me about Fern," Ry says.

"I was?" Lawrence Welk says, and then he does.

Fern

Lawrence Welk had surgery, to remove his tonsils, because he thought it would impress a girl, a nurse, named Fern. She became his wife, eventually, but not because of the surgery.

When he wrote her love letters he used a dictionary.

Lawrence Welk was impressed by Fern because she seemed unimpressed by him.

"Who's he?" Fern asked, when Lawrence Welk asked her if she wanted to go see a performance by Louis Armstrong.

They were married at five thirty in the morning.

Fern usually couldn't come to Lawrence Welk's shows.

Or was it that she could, but she didn't want to.

"Please don't make us move again," is something Fern liked to say right before Lawrence Welk made them move again.

When Fern asked Lawrence Welk to stop traveling, and find them a home, he bought them a hotel to live in, which Fern then ended up taking care of, when Lawrence Welk then went back on the road.

Silence

On the television, team handball, the Danish Superliga, from Aalborg. The sound is off. There is no quieter place on earth than a motel room where the television is playing with sound off.

Good Idea

"That's probably a good idea," says Ry, when Lawrence Welk tells him he should probably check in with Fern.

Checking In

"Lawrence," Fern says. He can hear her, but he can't see her. Everything is dark, and foul. It's as though he's wearing the goshawk's leather hood. "Lawrence," Fern says again, and Lawrence Welk knows what she's going to say, because Ry has just told him what Ry's wife had said to him, and now Fern more-or-less says it to Lawrence Welk. "I don't think you need to check in with me anymore."

Heaven Is . . . ?

"Is heaven a place you spend eternity with the people you love, or is it a place where you get to start over?" Ry asks. Lawrence Welk picks up a pillow and threatens to strike Ry in the face with it, and Ry puts his hands up and says, "Hey, what? It's an interesting question."

Heaven Is . . .

For Lawrence Welk, heaven was a place where you had time to let your mind wander, until it eventually stopped wandering and started thinking about what life was like before you went to heaven.

Eternity

Lawrence Welk asks Ry to tell him what divorce is like. Ry takes a deep pull from his joint, squints against the burn, exhales, and says, "Divorce, man, it's forever."

Rules

Lawrence Welk calls Ry's father, wakes him up, says that he needs to go back to heaven. Ry's father sighs. Lawrence Welk can picture him, lying in bed, running his hand over his face. "OK," Ry's father says, "here's the deal. If you win the election, you stay in North Dakota. If you lose the election, then you go back to heaven. Those are the rules."

So that is what Lawrence Welk will do. He will lose the election and go back to heaven and try to work things out with Fern.

"You mean you'll intentionally lose the election?" Ry's father asks and Lawrence Welk says yes. Ry's father takes a long time to respond. Lawrence Welk knows that the longer it takes someone to speak, the less likely it is you're going to want to hear what they have to say.

"Then you won't get to go back to heaven," Ry's father says. Why not? Lawrence Welk wants to know. Ry's father has told him some of the rules; now Lawrence Welk wants to know the rest of them. But Ry's father can't tell him. Or he can, but he doesn't want to.

Q and A

But of course Lawrence Welk knows that Ry's father has not made the rules. Ry's father is a man, and men follow rules that are made my God.

"Can you make an exception to the rule?" Lawrence Welk asks God.

No one answers.

"Why have you forsaken me?" he asks God.

No one answers.

How do you know you've been forsaken?

When no one answers.

Breakfast Included

The terror of the sleepless night in the Econolodge. The terror of Fern. The terror of her not needing him. The terror of her not thinking about him. The terror of having to tell the children that they've split up. The terror of losing and not ever seeing or talking to his children again. The terror of his children, who were born in states that were not North Dakota, dying and going to a heaven that is not his. The terror of his children dying. The terror of the next day's poll numbers, the feedback of the microphone at the presser, the bored hostility of the crowds, the loneliness, the loneliness, the breakfast buffet in the hotel lobby, the scratched plastic top over the platter of minimuffins, the hot-to-the-touch metal bin of hashbrowns, the splutteringly empty carafe of houseblend.

On Second Thought

Ry, with his eye dropper raised like a baton over Lawrence Welk's cup of orange juice. Lawrence Welk nods and Ry squeezes and a drop of the liquid lingers for a second before it plunks into the juice.

Treat Yourself

They pull into Beulah in a sports car. A red Miata, convertible, from Enterprise. The top is down. Ry was against it. The car is foreign made. It is thirty-two degrees out and the clouds, finally, say snow. But Lawrence

Welk insisted. He says folks like to see politicians wave as they come through town. There are no people on the sidewalks. There are no sidewalks. There are people, but they're in their own cars, which are not convertibles and their windows are up. Lawrence Welk waves anyway. He waves and waves, and the wind feels like it's about to lift the top of his head right off. Agreeably so. Lawrence Welk has always had a weakness for convertibles and has always been able to figure out some reason why he should have one.

High

In the Miata, parked outside the Crossroads Assisted Living Facility. Lawrence Welk asks Ry what day it is and Ry says Tuesday and Lawrence Welk asks, "What day is Tuesday?"

Low

"All days are the same in heaven," Lawrence Welk answers. In response to a question about what a typical Tuesday is like in heaven, asked by a ravaged, croaking, sunken-in-her-wheelchair resident of the Crossroads Assisted Living Facility. Where all days are also the same.

Now and Then

"You used to make me want to dance," the woman says.

"And now?" Lawrence Welk asks. He wants her to say, "And now, you make me want to vote for you." But a minute goes by and she doesn't say that, or anything. Because she has fallen asleep. Which must be what Lawrence Welk makes her want to do now.

Ideation

"Do you ever feel like there's a rope hanging over your head?" asks Ry.

They're on their way to return the Miata.

"I wonder what it would feel like to drive off a bridge," Ry wonders. As they're driving the Miata over a bridge.

What Next?

An hour later the Miata is returned and they're back in their motel room. Ry is sitting crosslegged on the floor. He asks, "What do we do now?"

Lawrence Welk is standing; if I sit down, he wonders, will I ever get back up? He feels disgusting. Like he's drowning in a huge vat of tapioca pudding that he's tried and failed to eat his way out of. The latest poll numbers are terrible. There is a hole in the toe of Lawrence Welk's left sock. No wonder Fern doesn't want me to check in with her anymore, he thinks.

And then he thinks, Enough.

Ry has a gummy in each hand. Red, in the shape of a dancing bear. He puts one in his mouth and offers Lawrence Welk the other. Lawrence Welk shakes his head, smooths back his hair, tugs on his lapels.

"There's only one thing to do," Lawrence Welk says.

"Give up," Ry guesses, and Lawrence Welk says no.

"Complain," Ry says.

"Never complain," Lawrence Welk says. When Ry asks why, Lawrence Welk answers, "People who complain rarely get over the habit."

Ry tries again. "Find someone to blame," he says.

"Who?"

"Our fucking wives. Those . . ." Lawrence Welk leans over and slaps Ry before he can finish the sentence. Hard, across the left cheek with his right hand. Lawrence Welk must still be high because it seems as though with the blow Ry's cheek expands and contracts, like an accordion. Ry must still be high, too: He acts as though he hasn't been struck at all. He doesn't even rub his cheek.

"So what *do* we do then?" he wants to know. Lawrence Welk extends his left hand. It is gnarled with veins and spots. Gross. That's one way to look at it. It is a hand that has lived and died and is now living again, living to help people get back on their feet! That's another way to look at it. Ry takes the hand and Lawrence Welk hauls him to his feet, and tells Ry, "We just keep trying to improve."

Humility

At twenty-five years old Lawrence Welk was being billed as America's Foremost Accordionist.

Said Lawrence Welk, "If I had any humility then, it certainly didn't show!"

Which is itself an expression of humility.

During that same time, he also sold candy between sets.

During that same time, he also performed in murder-mystery comedy sketches, and was praised as being the best corpse people had ever seen.

Once, when Lawrence Welk wanted to celebrate, he went out and bought thirty years' worth of underwear.

Lawrence Welk only hired musicians who were better than he was.

"I have never been an innovator, a creative genius," Lawrence Welk liked to say about himself.

When Lawrence Welk overheard another musician say he'd quit the music business if he had to play with an accordionist like Lawrence Welk, Lawrence Welk thought, "No, I can't be that bad!"

Lawrence Welk was told by another musician, "You're good. However, there's great room for improvement!"

Folks

Backstage, the middle school gymnasium in Valley City. Ry separates the curtains, peeks out. Lawrence Welk looks over Ry's shoulder. There are more than fifty people out there. Several of them are holding homemade signs. This seems like progress.

"Do you ever look at these people," Ry asks, "and think, Wow, they voted for a dead man."

Lawrence Welk *has* thought that, but instead he says, "Never call people 'people.' Always call them 'folks.' If you call them 'people' it makes them think you think you're better than them. But if you call them 'folks' it makes them think you're people, just like them."

Two Kinds

Lawrence Welk tells the crowd that there are two kinds of North Dakotans in heaven: those who constantly talk about moving to a warmer heaven, and those who think about all those more crowded, popular heavens and just can't understand how people can stand to be in heaven there.

The crowd laughs, and Lawrence Welk smiles, and the crowd laughs again.

Lawrence Welk always smiles. But when he *smiles*, he *really* smiles.

Memes

Lawrence Welk riding a bucking bronc. Lawrence Welk sitting in the electric chair. Lawrence Welk at gunpoint. Lawrence Welk's head bobbing in a sea of bubbling lava. Lawrence Welk getting a prostate exam. Lawrence Welk being held upside down by a professional wrestler, a man in purple tights, bare chested, hair of wheat. The man's breasts are enormous, tan, glistening. They are hairless. So are the man's legs. Lawrence Welk's head dangles between the man's legs, a big smile on his face. In all of the pictures, Lawrence has that same big smile on his face. He's smiling the way Ry has told him not to smile. Although Ry seems to be reconsidering. Lawrence Welk has gone viral, Ry tells him, as though sharing excellent news.

"What is this?" Lawrence Welk says to Ry, who is showing all these pictures on his phone.

"What do you mean?" Ry says. "It's you."

Second Debate

They are talking about the sanctity of marriage. How did they come to be talking about this? The moderator had asked them a question about soybean tariffs. Lawrence Welk's opponent does not have strong opinions about soybean tariffs, but he does have strong opinions about marriage. He gestures to his wife, who is sitting in the audience. She looks like a larger woman who has shrunk. Not that she has lost weight. But that she has been boiled down, or left too long in the clothes dryer. On her head is a baseball hat. She wears the hat forwards, and on the front is an image of her husband wearing his baseball hat backwards.

"We have a normal, healthy marriage," the opponent says. He leers at his wife and says, "A *very* healthy marriage, if you know what I mean."

Of course Lawrence Welk knows what he means. "What do you mean?" Lawrence Welk asks. His opponent insists Lawrence Welk knows exactly what he means. Lawrence Welk insists he really does not. Finally, goaded into it, the opponent says what he means, in great detail. Lawrence Welk watches the audience turn against his opponent as they listen to what he says. Although Lawrence Welk himself doesn't listen to what he says. Lawrence Welk doesn't like to hear about, or think about, or see certain bodily functions. He once watched a horse defecate on the street during a parade and in his memoir said not that the horse had defecated on the street but that it had "disgraced itself."

Instead, Lawrence Welk thinks about his bedroom in heaven. He'd slept there for three years before Fern died and joined him. On earth they'd always slept in the same bed. But in heaven, they slept in separate twins. Back on earth, they'd kiss each other goodnight; in heaven, they waved to each other goodnight from across the room. It could make you sad. Or you could find it sweet. Lawrence Welk finds it sweet. Or found it sweet, past tense, and that's when he realizes that that part of his life, or afterlife, is over. From his place on the stage, he looks at Fern waving at him from her bed as though from a great distance. I've known that lovely young lady for so long, Lawrence Welk thinks. What a wonderful thing to be waved at by her before we turn out the lights.

Champagne Ladies

Lawrence Welk told one young woman that she was appalling.

Appealing is what he meant to tell her she was.

Lawrence Welk's male band members were forbidden to date any of the female singers. Although some of them did it anyway.

"Champagne Ladies" is what Lawrence Welk called his female singers.

One of whom he fired for wearing skirts that were too short, at least as far as Lawrence Welk was concerned.

And three others he let go for wanting to be paid what they were worth, although Lawrence Welk disagreed that, as Champagne Ladies, they were worth that much at all.

"A sweetheart to all, a sweetheart to none" is what Lawrence Welk called his ideal Champagne Lady.

Reckoning

At the monthly meeting of the North Dakota Association for Women in Business. On the fourteen floor of a glass tower in Grand Forks. Lawrence Welk can't believe there's a building this tall and this glassy in North Dakota, nor can he believe that there are this many women in business in North Dakota.

They've asked him to come to their meeting to address their concerns regarding his past comments and actions toward women.

Ry is standing at the back of the room, looking nervous. He's coached Lawrence Welk, told Lawrence Welk that he should say: "It's clear that I have a lot of work to do. And I'm going to do that starting right now—not by talking, but by listening."

Lawrence Welk has nothing against listening, or working. But is listening work? Not for a musician. As far as Lawrence Welk is concerned, a musician, at work, plays, so that others, at play, can listen.

"Trust me," Ry told him. "This is what you're supposed to say. So just say it." And Lawrence Welk wants to trust Ry, and so he says it.

The women in the room say nothing, but the temperature in the room changes, goes from somewhat cool to very cold and also very hot, as when thunder breaks out during a snowstorm. Charged, in other words. Dangerous, in other words. It reminds Lawrence Welk of that moment right before Lawrence Welk's saxophonist was stabbed in the stomach for smiling at a pretty girl in the audience at Devil's Lake. And after that, Lawrence Welk tells the North Dakota Association of Women in Business, he, Lawrence Welk, made extra sure to be very careful about what girls he smiled at.

Endorsement from the North Dakota Association of Women in Business

"We could vote for no one. But we really want to vote for someone."

First Thought/Best Thought

". . . But if you call them 'folks' it makes them think you're people, just like them," Ry tells his father. It's their nightly state-of-the-campaign telephone powwow. Bedtime stories. Broken curfews. What is life but a series of tense nighttime conversations with your father?

"Thanks," Ry says after his father praises his theory of folks.

"Of course I came up with that on my own," Ry says after his father asks whether he came up with the theory on his own.

Cover Songs

Apologetic. Is what Ry is when he realizes that Lawrence Welk has heard him pass off Lawrence Welk's theory of folks as his own. But Lawrence Welk says not to apologize. All of his best songs, he tells Ry, were somebody else's songs first.

Let Me Entertain You

When given the opportunity to play on the radio, Lawrence Welk agreed, even though he worried that he wouldn't know how to play on the radio.

When Lawrence Welk first started playing songs on the radio, he would stomp on the floor so loudly that someone in the studio finally gave him a pillow to put under his foot

Lawrence Welk used his band to sell bubble gum. To sell beer. To sell cars. Vitamins. Sleeping pills. Aftershave. Mobile homes. And also, of course, to play good music.

"The prime purpose of entertainers," Lawrence Welk says, "is to entertain and give the audience what it wants, always consistent with basic moral standards."

Lawrence Welk doesn't sing. But he likes it when other people sing.

When is Lawrence Welk happy? When other people are happy.

ICU

"Don't forget, you're here to ask for their vote," says Ry, as they walk into the hospital at Jamestown.

"Why are you here?" a nurse, Betty H. says, as she admits them into the ICU. They are in the hall. On either side of the hall, a series of open doors. Lawrence Welk is holding his accordion, which, as he begins to exercise it, writhes and wheezes like a living thing.

Everywhere, from every room, are the sounds and the smells of very sick people. And then the terrible hum of the hospital machinery. Why is the sound of hospital machinery—the machinery that keeps you alive—more terrible than the sound of other machinery?

Ry's face is suddenly as white as Betty H.'s uniform. He is like a lot of healthy people: He's spent most of his life acting like it's no big deal to be very sick. He whispers to Lawrence Welk, "Don't tell her you're here for their vote." But Lawrence never had any intention of telling Betty H. that he was here for their vote.

"I'm here," Lawrence Welk says, "to entertain them."

Lawrence Welk plays a few notes on his accordion, and already Betty H. recognizes the song. From the Thanksgiving Day Special broadcast. 1970. Which Betty H. watched and listened to in syndication in April 1996, in the den of her Aunt Terry's house in Gascoyne. Aunt Terry in her easy chair, Betty H. in her uncle Matt's recliner. Uncle Matt was dead. He had never liked Lawrence Welk anyway. On their laps were TV trays. On them, plates, and on the plates, grilled cheese sandwiches. The cheese was Velveeta. What has happened to Velveeta? What has happened to those TV trays? What has happened to Aunt Terry?

"What's more American than cornflakes?" Betty H. sings, from memory. "What's more American than toothpaste? I am, I am, I am!"

The song is over. From some of the rooms, faint applause. A weak wolf whistle. "Oh, oh!" someone says from one of the rooms. It is appreciation or pain? Lawrence Welk knows he has done something. But what has he done? And has it been enough?

Questions

Reporter: Are you going to vote for Lawrence Welk?

Woman on the Street: You know, I think I am.

Reporter: Why?

Woman on the Street: I don't know. His music, I guess.

Reporter: You like his music?

Woman on the Street: His music is horrible, but it helps.

Children

Lawrence Welk did not spank his children. But he would talk to them about what they'd done wrong until they begged him to spank them.

Lawrence Welk and Fern were apart when their first child was born. A girl. Shirley. Five pounds, twelve ounces, Lawrence Welk was told over the phone. But all Lawrence Welk heard was "five ounces."

"Do you think she has a chance?" Lawrence Welk wanted to know.

Lawrence Welk's daughter kept biting the girl next door. So, Lawrence Welk built a fence around their house, to keep their daughter in, the girl next door out.

But Shirley enticed the girl next door to stick her hand through the slats, and she did that, and then Shirley bit her hand.

"Daddy's not a good fisherman. But he's very good for putting worms on your line," Shirley once said.

Checking In

"Lawrence" is how Fern begins this conversation, just as she began their last one. Although this time it's she who is checking in with him.

Lawrence Welk and Ry are in their motel room, prepping for one of his last campaign stops. Ry points at the door, and then at himself, and then at the door again, but Lawrence Welk shakes his head. It is good to have company, even if the company is aggravating. For the first time, he understands what Fern sees in the goshawk.

Speaking of the goshawk, in the distance Lawrence Welk sees the bird in midair, battling with another bird. There is something beautiful about birds in flight fighting, although Lawrence Welk guesses that's not necessarily so if you're one of the birds.

Fern is looking at the birds through binoculars while balancing on a unicycle. The unicycle's tire is enormous and it has enormous studs. The snow is midwheel-high. Fern is balancing on a big-tired unicycle in the snow while looking through binoculars at a bird that is nearly impossible to train that she has trained. There are people who are happy when things are easy. Fern, Lawrence Welk realizes, has become a person who is happiest when she's doing something more difficult than the last difficult thing she did.

Or maybe she was always this way. Back on earth, Fern was a champion duplicate bridge player. She would sometimes change partners, from tournament to tournament. Often she replaced superior partners with lesser ones. Lawrence Welk had always assumed that the replaced partners had done something to make Fern dislike them. But maybe, it occurs to him now, Fern just wanted to see if she could also win with the lesser ones.

Fern takes the binoculars away from her face. There are rings around her eyes from the binoculars. But she blinks and then smiles and then her eyes go back to normal.

"You're going to win this thing, aren't you?" she says.

"It's hard to say," Lawrence Welk says. "One poll says yes and one poll says no."

"Yes," Fern says. "But the poll that says no is an out-of-state poll."

Which means that Fern has been paying attention to the polls. Which means that Fern has been paying attention.

"You're going win this thing," Fern says, "and then you're going to see our children again, you lucky duck."

"You could see them, too," Lawrence says, and Fern grimaces, shakes her head, and looks sad. When she looks sad, she also looks, for a second, older. More Lawrence Welk's age than her own. "I don't think so," she says. "There are rules, you know."

"Come on, humor a sad old man," Lawrence Welk says, and that makes Fern laugh and then suddenly Lawrence Welk doesn't feel old or sad anymore. His heart leaps, like the goshawk at the throat of the other bird, which cries, and then begins to drop.

"You *are* going to win this thing," Fern says to Lawrence Welk, and then wheels off in the direction of the falling bird and is gone.

Speculative

"What if I win?" Lawrence Welk asks Ry. "Will Fern come back if I win?"

"Come back to you?"

"Come back here. To North Dakota. Where I'll be."

"How would that happen?" Ry wants to know.

"How has *this* happened?" Lawrence Welk wants to know. He allows his hands to travel the length of his torso, the way so many of his Champagne Ladies used to do when appearing in their most beautiful gowns. "Get a load of this," they communicated with their hands, and that is what Lawrence Welk is communicating with his. Then, he laughs, and Ry laughs, and says, "Well, I *guess* it could happen," and then sort of fake punches Lawrence Welk on the shoulder. Lawrence Welk is surprised by how warm this makes him feel. "I've just started my second life," Lawrence Welk thinks, "and already, I've made my first friend."

God

"I shall ignore your prayers. I shall never respond to them. If you ask me a question, I shall never answer it. And in that way, you shall never know what is not possible."

Home Team

The biggest crowd yet, in the Fargo municipal ice arena. Lawrence Welk is standing on the red carpet. Overhead are two banners. One banner communicates that the team won the central division of the Upper Midwest Hockey League in 2017. WE ARE THE SKYHAWKS!!!! says the other banner. The Skyhawks? What other kind of hawk is there? The assistant general manager hands Lawrence Welk a T-shirt. On it, an image of a bird, standing, not flying, with a cigar in its mouth. He accepts the T-shirt. He will give it to Fern, if he sees her again. If she doesn't like it, she can give it to the goshawk. Lawrence Welk thanks the assistant general manager and then says what he is there to say. At the end of his speech he says, "Go Skyhawk-ah!" The crowd roars. The players hold their mouthguards in one hand, rattle their sticks against the boards with the other.

Snow! Snow! Snow!

Finally, it is snowing. The flakes whirling in the high distant lights of the Best Western parking lot. Lawrence Welk is six feet tall. How long would it have to snow, how long would Lawrence Welk would have to stand there, until he was buried by the snow? Too long. Once, he slept on a couch on a porch, and it snowed overnight, six inches, and he didn't wake up until the next morning. What a feeling that was to wake up under all that soft cold! What a wonder it was to sit up and watch the snow slide away from him! He lies down, on the parking lot. Meanwhile, Ry is the room, propped up in bed with his shoes still on, talking on his phone, watching a cooking show on TV with the sound off.

Iowa

Lawrence Welk walks back to the room and overhears Ry talking on the phone with his father. Lawrence Welk is not eavesdropping. The door is open, even though it's snowing out. And the phone is on speaker. That is the key to every election, Lawrence Welk is learning. People want to be heard.

Apparently, Ry's father says, other states' Democratic chairmen are impressed by what Ry's done with Lawrence Welk. And Lawrence Welk thinks: *With*? Is that the proper preposition? What have you done *with* me?

"Iowa has a house race coming up," Ry's father says. He names the presumed frontrunner. "They want you to run her campaign." Ry's father asks if Ry knows what happened to the person who managed the last successful Democrat run for senate in Iowa?

"Wisconsin," Ry says. He says it in a way that hurts Lawrence Welk's heart. He says it in the way that Lawrence Welk had once said the name of the bigger ballroom than the one he was playing in, and the next bigger ballroom after that, and so on, and so on, until he started saying, in a different way, the names of the ballrooms that were smaller than the one he was playing in.

Goodbye, Ry

If he won, Lawrence Welk had been planning on asking Ry to be his chief of staff. But of course Lawrence Welk doesn't tell Ry that now.

Because Lawrence Welk has always believed that if someone wants to leave, then you should make it easy for them to leave.

"Two more days and you get your life back!" he says. Ry is red faced, guilty-seeming. He knows Lawrence Welk has heard the phone conversation. He opens his mouth to apologize, but before he can Lawrence Welk snaps off the TV and tells Ry, "Let's get to it!" The last debate is tomorrow and they have work to do.

Last Debate

His opponent is better prepared for this debate than the others. He's seen the poll numbers, too. And maybe he doesn't want to go back to heaven. He calmly, deliberately, goes through each of Lawrence Welk's proposals, each of his position papers, each of his pledge promises, and shows how farfetched they are. "He's making promises he can't keep," the opponent says.

The moderator asks if Lawrence Welk would like to respond and Lawrence Welk nods and says to his opponent, "You're right-ah!" Because what is music, happy music, but a promise that you cannot keep?

Then Lawrence Welk smiles. So widely that it seems like the smile might take over his face. He can't help it. Yes, he can. He doesn't want to help it. He is having fun. "If you look like you're having fun," Lawrence Welk has always said, "then folks will, too." His opponent is not having fun. He turns his hat around and Lawrence Welk watches the vein in his forehead bulge and beat. It reminds him of a song. A complicated song. Played by musicians more talented than Lawrence Welk. The opponent takes a step toward him. Lawrence Welk knows his opponent might hit him, depending on what he says next. Lawrence Welk knows that his opponent might hit him, no matter what Lawrence Welk says next. So Lawrence Welk says what he wants to say.

"Folks," he says to the people in the audience, and to the people watching on their TVs, "I'm just happy to be home again, and alive."

RECKONINGS

I saw a headline on the internet that read, "White People Need to Reckon with Atticus Finch's Racism."

What did I remember about Atticus Finch? That he was a character in a novel I read back in middle school called *To Kill a Mockingbird.* What else did I remember about Atticus Finch? Not a lot. I'd read the book thirty-seven years ago, and thirty-seven years is a long time to remember a book, or anything.

So I found the phone number of my eighth-grade English teacher, Mr. Crawford, and then called him. He didn't pick up, and so I left a voicemail message for him that said, "Mr. Crawford, it's Russell Johnson. Long time no see! I have some questions for you, about Atticus Finch. Please call me back."

After I hung up, I felt aimless, empty, like I should be doing something, something fulfilling. But what? I looked at my dog, Maude, lying at my feet. And then I typed into my phone, "Atticus Finch dog." The first thing that popped up was the question "Why did Atticus Finch shoot the dog?"

I was inside, looking outside. It was a beautiful day out there! Everything was in its proper place. The sun was in the sky, the birds were in the trees, and my across-the-street neighbor, Mike, was sitting on his front steps, smoking a cigarette and looking at his phone. Sitting next to him was his own dog, Legend.

I leaned out my window and said, "Hey Mike, did you know that Atticus Finch shot a dog?"

Mike looked up from his phone and said, through his cigarette, "Yeah, *fuck* that guy." He spat his cigarette into the street, scrambled to his feet, and then charged back into his house, Legend right behind him.

I'd lived across the street from Mike for seven years, had small-talked with him pretty much every day. I knew he loved his dog, and dogs in general, and also people who loved dogs. "I don't *get* a person who doesn't love a dog," he'd once told me. And I knew that he, like me, did something with computers for a living, I didn't know exactly what, but I did know that, whatever it was, he could and did do it from his home. But what else did I know? Not much. He'd never been in my house, and I'd never been in his. Close your eyes, Russell, I told myself, and try to picture what Mike's house looks like on the inside. I did that, but all I could picture was Legend sitting next to Mike while Mike did something on his computer.

While my eyes were already closed, I thought I might as well try to picture Mr. Crawford. I hadn't seen him in thirty-seven years, but there he was, standing in front of the classroom, his pear-shaped body in a threadbare blue business suit that was too short in the sleeves. Mr. Crawford was bald. While he lectured, he liked to put his hand on the back of his head, fingers up, like rooster feathers, and then let them fall to his bald head, one by one, pinky first, thumb last.

"Hey, Mr. Crawford," I said, the way you do when you walk into a teacher's classroom, and then my phone rang, and it was him.

"You have questions about Atticus," Mr. Crawford said. I remembered this about him: that he referred to characters in books by their first names, although he referred to his students by their last.

"I do," I said.

"As well you should, Johnson," Mr. Crawford said. "His book is a cabinet of mysteries, provocations, comforts, and wonders. Tell me what you remember about it."

"Not a lot," I admitted.

"*That* I find difficult to believe," Mr. Crawford said. His voice sounded faint, barely there. How *old* are you? I wanted to ask. But then, I'd wanted to ask him that question thirty-seven years ago, too.

"It's been thirty-seven years," I pointed out.

"There is no time when it comes to literature," Mr. Crawford. "All the clocks were thrown out of heaven."

And what did *that* mean? It sounded like a quote. Was it a quote from *To Kill a Mockingbird*? I typed "to kill a mockingbird clocks heaven" and the first hit was for high quality clocks inspired by *To Kill a Mockingbird* and made by independent artists. But the link didn't say anything about heaven, and didn't say anything about *To Kill a Mockingbird*, either, except that the independent artists had been inspired by it to make high quality clocks.

Meanwhile, Mr. Crawford was waiting for me to tell him what I remembered about *To Kill a Mockingbird*. "Do your best, Johnson," he said, which is what he always said when he was pretty sure your best wasn't going to be good enough.

I tried. Atticus Finch, I told Mr. Crawford, was a judge, who had children, three of them, one of them was a boy named Harper. I couldn't remember the names of the other two, although I knew one of them had been based on a real-life person who later became famous, although I didn't remember the real-life person's name, either. The book was set in Mississippi, and in it Atticus Finch was the judge for the trial of a falsely accused black man, whose name was Boo Radley. It was murder he was falsely accused of, but Atticus Finch ruled that Boo Radley was innocent and he was freed. The end.

Then I stopped talking and waited for Mr. Crawford to tell me what I'd gotten wrong. I knew there was probably something. But Mr. Crawford didn't say anything, at first. His breath came in rapid puffs out of his mouth, through the phone, into my ear.

"The book is set in Alabama," he finally said, in a bored voice. "Atticus Finch was not a judge. He was a lawyer. The famous person was the writer Truman Capote, who was the basis for the character Dill, who was not Atticus Finch's child, but a friend of his children. His children were Jem and Scout. Scout is the narrator. She is a girl. Harper, Harper Lee, was not a boy and she was not a character in the novel. She was the author of the novel. Boo Radley was a white man, the specter next door, with whom the children are obsessed. The black man was named Tom Robinson. He *was* falsely accused, but of rape, not murder. And he was convicted, and sent to prison, and then he was killed trying to escape from prison. Those are the *facts*, Johnson. It's startling that you don't recall them, but then we don't read novels for *facts*. We read novels for what they make us think, and how they make us feel. When someone asks you what you remember about a novel, they are not asking you what facts you remember; they are asking you to remember what it made you think and how it made you feel. Now I will ask you again: Tell me, Johnson, *what do you remember about* To Kill a Mockingbird?"

Again, I tried. I tried to remember what the novel had made me think, and how it had made me feel. And again, I couldn't remember much. "Actually," I told Mr. Crawford, "what I really wanted to know is whether you think Atticus Finch is a racist."

Again, Mr. Crawford didn't respond right away. I couldn't even hear him breathing. He made no noise at all for one second, then another, then several more. I was starting to wonder if he was still on the phone, or alive, until finally he sighed, one big long *whoosh*. "Johnson," Mr. Crawford said, "I want you to listen very carefully to this," and then he hung up.

Here's why no one likes to talk on the phone anymore: because it hurts to be hung up on. Is there a more violent feeling of emptiness than being hung up on? Probably. And then, since you've been hung up on, you have the time, the occasion, to think of those more violent feelings of emptiness, and I did, and then I didn't want to think of them anymore, and so I looked at my phone again and on it I saw those high quality clocks that had been inspired by *To Kill a Mockingbird* and made by independent artists. So I bought one. My phone congratulated me on my purchase and said the clock—my clock—would be delivered to my home within the hour by Instant Express Delivery.

Maude and I went out to my front porch to enjoy the sun and wait for my clock to show up, and while we did two things happened.

First, Mike emerged from his house, followed by Legend. Both seemed worked up. Legend circled Mike while Mike attacked his phone with his thumbs. A cigarette was in his mouth, but it was not yet lit. "What's that dog killer's name again?" Mike shouted—into his phone,

I thought, at first, but when his phone didn't answer and Mike looked up, I realized he was shouting at me.

"You mean Atticus?" I said, and immediately felt this warm feeling come up, through my stomach and throat and into my face, and I understood then why Mr. Crawford referred to his beloved characters by their first names: because when you call someone from a book by their first name it signifies that you really know them. You would never call a character by their first name if you didn't know them, intimately. Whereas you can call someone by their first name in the world, outside a book, and still not really know them at all. Mike, for instance.

Anyway, Mike nodded. "Atticus Rich, right?" he said, and started tapping something into his phone again. I know now that he was searching for a person named Atticus Rich in our city. There was one. Mike found him, found a way to communicate with him through the usual open channels. I hear you're a dog killer, Mike said, or typed, to Atticus Rich. Atticus Rich said he wasn't, but on the other hand, so what if he was? How was it any business of Mike's? Who the hell was Mike? Who the hell did Mike think he was? They spoke, or typed, back and forth to each other like this, escalating, escalating, until Mike had enough, and went out and found Atticus Rich and shot and killed him.

I couldn't have known all that at the time. But I could have corrected Mike when he said Atticus's last name. "Atticus *Finch*," I could have told him. "Not *Rich*." And I would have, or I might have, and that would have changed everything, or almost everything, except that the other thing happened: I got a phone call—not from Mr. Crawford, but from Ms. Hardaway, my eighth-grade guidance counselor.

"Se*ñ*or Johnson," she said, by way of greeting, and I remembered this about her: that when she talked with students, she would occasionally use Spanish words and phrases. One rumor was that before she'd become a guidance counselor she'd been a Spanish teacher, or that she'd worked for the Peace Corps in a Spanish-speaking country. Another rumor was that she was high all the time. I tried to picture her, with my eyes open this time, and there she was: in her tiny, windowless office, with an oriental rug taking up most of the floor, sitting in an enormous, cushioned wicker chair that took up most of the office. Hanging from her neck by a chain was a pair of glasses that she never put on her face. Her eyes were watery blue and all her clothes were much too big for her. It was like she was being swarmed by her clothes rather than wearing them. "Mr. Crawford said you might be having a little problem."

"I couldn't remember anything about *To Kill a Mockingbird*," I admitted. "Plus, I wanted to know if Mr. Crawford thought Atticus Finch was a racist."

Ms. Hardaway clucked her tongue—in sympathy, it sounded like, although I couldn't tell if it was in sympathy for me, or Mr. Crawford.

"That is between you and Mr. Crawford," Ms. Hardaway said. "That is a book, and a book is a thing that is outside my jurisdiction."

"Your jurisdiction?"

"Yes, my jurisdiction. My purview."

I tried to remember if I'd known, thirty-seven years ago, that Ms. Hardaway had had a purview, or even if I knew, thirty-seven years ago, what a purview was. But no, those things, like certain important details about what and how Atticus Finch and *To Kill a Mockingbird* made me think and feel, were also lost in the mist of time. "What *is* your purview?"

"My purview is that which you will become. My purview is your future. Which, thirty-seven years after you left my presence, is now your present."

Just then a boxy, yellow van pulled up in front of my house. On its side was the legend Instant Express Delivery. A man in yellow shorts and a yellow, short-sleeve shirt emerged from the van holding a brown box. He trotted up my stairs, handed me the box, and said, "Here you go." The man then reached into his pocket, pulled out a dog treat, said "Here *you* go," and then tossed the treat to Maude, who caught and ate it with a *snap*. The man patted her on the head, descended the stairs, hopped back into his van, and disappeared with a puff of exhaust and a toot of his horn.

"What was that?" Ms. Hardaway asked.

"I got a package."

"Yes, that is a thing we all get now," Ms. Hardaway said. "We all get packages. That is the human condition."

"It is?" I said. I quickly looked it up on my phone, and then read Ms. Hardaway the first definition I found there. "The human condition," I told her, "is the characteristics, key events, and situations which compose the essentials of human existence, such as birth, growth, emotionality, aspiration, conflict, mortality."

"In other words," Ms. Hardaway said, "a package." She paused, and then asked, "What kind of package?"

"It's a clock," I said. "I got it . . ."

"Never mind," Ms. Hardaway interrupted. "I shouldn't have asked. It doesn't matter what kind of package, or why you got it. Only that you got one. That is one of the only two things that matters."

"What's the other thing?" I asked.

"1981," Ms. Hardaway said, and I heard the sound of pages being flipped. "In 1981, June 5th, the week before you were to graduate middle school and move on to high school—which, as you remember, was just across the street—you and I conducted an exit interview. We did not call it an exit interview then, but that was what we would and do call it now. Do you remember that?"

"I do," I said, but I really didn't. I mean, I could see Ms. Hardaway, in her office, and I could even see her mouth moving, but I couldn't hear or remember what came out of it. All this not-remembering was starting to scare me a little. Try, Russell, I told myself. Try what? I asked myself back, because I couldn't remember what I'd been asking myself to try to do. So I looked at my phone. There on my phone, was the definition of the human condition, which was different than the one that Ms. Hardaway had come up with, which was also different than the one that I came up with, right there, which is this: The human condition is not being able to remember the thing you were thinking about before the most recent thing you were thinking about.

"You clearly don't," Ms. Hardaway said.

"Don't what?" I asked.

"Remember our exit interview," Ms. Hardaway said. She sighed and continued. "You were wearing a sweatshirt, green, with a prominent white, four-leaf clover on the chest. The sleeves had been cut off, not neatly, as though you'd cut them off with scissors using your weak hand, which, according to your file, was, and I assume still is, your left. Also, you were wearing gray sweatpants, and over those sweatpants, blue basketball shorts. A remarkable outfit, mi amigo." She paused, as though giving me the opportunity to remember. I did, now. Although I wonder if you can be said to remember something that someone else is remembering for you. "I commended you for completing your middle-school journey . . ."

". . . in style!" I said, because I suddenly recalled her using that phrase, and how corny it sounded, and how good it made me feel.

"That is what I said," Ms. Hardaway continued. "To you, and to approximately seventy-five percent of your graduating class. The upper seventy-five percent. To the lower twenty-five percent I said, 'Well, it's been a struggle, and there were moments, many moments, when I think we both wondered if you were going to make it through all three years of middle school, but you did it, and here we are.'"

"You actually said that?"

"Only to the lower twenty-five percent," Ms. Hardaway said. "To the upper seventy-five percent I congratulated them for completing their middle school journey in style, and then I asked them what they wanted to be when they grew up. Do you remember what you told me? No, of course you don't. No one ever remembers. Only one percent of the seventy-five percent remembers. A lawyer, hermanito, you wanted to be a lawyer when you grew up. When I asked you what kind of lawyer, you said, 'Wait there are different *kinds*?' Which I found touching. You with your absurd outfit and your stringy arms sticking out of those ragged sweatshirt holes and your three-year cumulative B+ grade point average and your surprisingly high score on the Iowa standardized test and that earnest look on your face. I wanted to hug you. But of course that was outside of my purview. *Well outside*. In any case, I did not hug you. Instead I told you that yes, there were many different kinds of lawyers. I named some of them, and you contemplated what I'd told you. While you contemplated you gnawed on the inside of your bottom lip. As did at least fifty percent of the top seventy five percent when thinking about their future. You gnawed *hard*, too, pobrecito. I worried that you were going to draw blood. But you didn't. Instead, you finally asked, 'What kind of lawyer is Atticus Finch?'"

"And what did you say?" I asked.

"I said," Ms. Hardaway said, "that Atticus Finch was in a book and as such was outside my purview. And the sad look on your face when I said that! Oh, I wanted to hug you again, real right. But I couldn't do that. As you know. So instead, I actually answered your question. I said, 'He was a lawyer who tried to do the right thing in a book.' I specified 'in a book' because I wanted to stress to you that a book is not the world, and what is possible in a book, or valued in a book, or wanted in a book, is not always, or even usually, possible or valued or wanted in the world, or for that matter what was possible or valued or wanted in a book when it was written would not necessarily be possible, valued, or wanted when it was read. This is why my esteemed colleagues in the English Department are so insistent that I stick to my purview. Not that you registered the distinction between the book and the world anyway. Only the top five percent can register than distinction, and only two percent of them even care. And do you remember what you said? No, of course you don't. But I do. You said something very sweet, something that gave me hope, something that I would have remembered, even had I not written it in your file, which I did. You said, 'Yeah, that's definitely the kind of lawyer I'm gonna be.'"

"I remember," I said, now that she'd helped me remember. I could see myself, too, in her office, after I'd said what Ms. Hardaway had reminded me I'd said. I was sitting in a folding metal chair, hunched over, elbows on my knees, looking at the oriental rug. Why? Because I'd felt sheepish that I'd said this big thing, made this big claim, voiced this big hope about my future. And because I meant it. I was sincere. And I was afraid that Ms. Hardaway would make fun of me. No, that's not it: I was afraid that she *wouldn't* make of fun of me, that she wouldn't say anything at all, but would instead think what I was thinking, which was this: I probably won't end up being that kind of lawyer, or any kind of lawyer, or any kind of thing anyone would really want to be when they grow up. So yes, I looked sheepish, and sad, then. Or maybe it was that

I felt sad, now, because I knew what question was coming next, and how I would answer it.

"Well?" Ms. Hardaway asked, and I could hear the flinch in her voice. "Have you become that kind of lawyer?" I told her I hadn't, that I hadn't become any kind of lawyer at all. "What *have* you become then?" she asked.

"I work from home, on my computer."

"You're a writer then?" she asked, her voice brighter now, and when I said yes, she said, "Thirty-seven years you asked me what kind of lawyer was Atticus Finch, and now I ask you, Russell, mi corazon palpitante: What kind of writer are you?"

"I write lists."

"Lists?"

"Lists." As I said this, I looked across the street. Mike and Legend had gone back inside his house and they were now coming out of it again. Mike was holding Legend's leash with his left hand, and a handgun with his right. He wasn't trying to hide it. He walked down the street, holding the gun like he didn't care who saw him, like it was legal to do so. Because it was legal, in our state. I knew this because one of the lists I'd written last week was Top Ten States for Gun Lovers. "Top Ten States for Gun Lovers," I told Ms. Hardaway. "Top Five Cities for Frozen Custard Fans," which was the list I'd written earlier that day. "Seven Reasons Not To Have Your Wisdom Teeth Extracted," which was the list I was planning to write tomorrow. "That kind of thing."

Ms. Hardaway didn't say anything. She didn't hang up, but she didn't say anything either. And this is another reason no one wants to talk on the phone anymore: A phone is a perfect vehicle for the communication of disappointment. You can express it by hanging up, and you can also express it by not saying anything at all. Just by holding the phone, in silence, can you make your feelings known.

"What kind of clock?" Ms. Hardaway finally asked. Her voice sounded tired. It suddenly felt like we'd been talking for a very long time.

"What's that?" I asked.

"Inside your package is a clock," Ms. Hardaway reminded me. "An alarm clock? Digital? Analog? A grandfather clock? A Kit-Cat clock? A cuckoo clock? Is it a cuckoo clock? I've always liked those. *That* is what I wanted to be when I grew up. Not a guidance counselor, but a maker of cuckoo clocks. That whimsical sound. That happy little bird."

"It's not a cuckoo clock," I said, and then told her what kind of clock it was. Again, there was silence, briefer this time, and then I heard the sound of something—my file, I guessed—slapping shut.

"That's outside my purview," Ms. Hardaway said, and then hung up.

I stared at the phone, like it had just insulted me. Then, I put it in my pocket, picked up the package. Maude got to her feet and followed me into the house. There, at the far end of the front hall, was a stack of packages, some of them opened, most of them not. I put this most recent package on top of the stack. I considered the stack, and felt so lost. What is even in those packages? I wondered. Why are they here? Why am *I* here? Why did I love *To Kill a Mockingbird* so much thirty-seven years ago? Why did I want to be like Atticus Finch? Why have I forgotten almost everything about it and him since then? Was he really a racist? Am I? What has happened to me? How did I get here?

How did I get here? A big question. The kind, I guess, you might turn to a book to help you answer. Maybe even a book like *To Kill a Mockingbird*. Except I didn't have *To Kill a Mockingbird*. But I did have my phone. A book and a phone have something in common. They both can tell you how you got here, but a phone can tell you a lot faster.

So I took my phone out of my pocket and went through my search history, back through the clock and the human condition and Mr. Crawford's phone number and Atticus Finch shooting the dog until, yes, there it was, the link that said that white people needed to reckon with Atticus Finch's racism.

So I clicked on the link and discovered that what I'd assumed would be an article arguing that white people like me needed to reckon with Atticus Finch's racism was instead an online course intended to teach white people like me how to reckon with Atticus Finch's racism. I took, and passed, the course, which was easy—the test didn't require that I read, or reread, the book. It just quoted passages in which Atticus Finch said, or did, something potentially racist, and then asked a series of multiple-choice questions about whether what he'd said or done was not racist, somewhat racist, or definitely racist. The answer to every question was "somewhat racist," except for the last question, which was, "Is being somewhat racist better than being definitely racist or just as bad as being definitely racist?" I suspected Atticus Finch would have said, "Better" and so I said, "Just as bad," and I got that one right, too—and then I felt much better, especially when I was told that within an hour I would receive, via Instant Express Delivery, a T-shirt that said I Reckoned with Atticus Finch's Racism.

I was about to pocket my phone and go out and wait on my front porch for my T-shirt to arrive when I noticed that between the time when I first saw the link and now, many links had popped up in response to the first link. "White People Have Many More Racist Things to Reckon with Than Atticus Finch's Racism" was one link. "If I Reckon with the Many Racist Things Do I Still Have to Reckon with Atticus Finch's Racism?" was another. "All People Need to Reckon with Atticus Finch's Racism" was a third. Followed by "Asking for a Friend: Do Asian Americans Also Need to Reckon with Atticus Finch's Racism?" and "Why Should Asian Americans Be Any Different than Other Americans?" and "A Brief History of Why Asian Americans Are Different than Other Americans" and "Other Americans: What You Will *Not* Find in *To Kill a Mockingbird*" and "There Is No Such Thing as an 'Other American'" and "How I Came to Embrace Being an 'Other American'" and "There Is a Case to Be Made That White Americans Are the Only 'Other Americans' but Is Anyone Brave Enough to Make It?" and "A Provocation: Atticus Finch Was the Only White American Brave Enough to Make the Case that White Americans Are the Only 'Other Americans'" and "A Sincere Question: Is There a Black Person on This Planet Named after Atticus Finch?" and "I Am a Black Person on This Planet Named after Atticus Finch" and "Another Sincere Question: Is There a Black Person on This Planet Not Adopted by White People Who Has Been Named after Atticus Finch?" and "I Loved My White Parents but I Would Have Loved Them More If They Hadn't Adopted Me" and "For Parents Only: How to Survive the Adoption Process" and "I Would Not Have Survived Being a Kid Without *To Kill a Mockingbird*" and "If I Had Known Being an Adult Would Be like This Then I Would Rather *Not* Have Survived Being a Kid" and "Ten Kids' Books That Make Childhood Worth Reading" and "Yes, Atticus Finch Is Racist and So Is *To Kill a Mockingbird* but That Doesn't Mean We Shouldn't Keep Reading It" and "An Inquiry: Want to Have It Both Ways Much?" and so on. There were too many links to mention, too many links to count, and definitely too many links to read. I scrolled down on my phone until I hit the most recent two links: "Does Anyone Really Give a Fuck About Atticus Finch and for That Matter Did Anyone Ever Really Give a Fuck About Atticus Finch?" and "My Eighth Grade Boyfriend Really Gave a Fuck About Atticus Finch and His Name Was Russell Johnson and I Wish He'd Get in Touch with Me and Here's the Link."

I clicked on the link. There was no one there, just the message that my host would be joining the meeting shortly. I was sitting at my desk which was also my kitchen table, and I put my phone down on the table, because my hands were shaking and I felt jittery—maybe from reading through all those links, or maybe because I couldn't remember who my eighth-grade girlfriend was. Think, Russell, think, I told myself, and then I did, and just in time I remembered her name—Cheryl Watterson!—and there she was on my phone, a white woman. I say that because she *was* a white woman, but also because this was one of the ways that the test had just helped me reckon with Atticus Finch's racism, which, for the most part, as far as the test was concerned, was synonymous with the book's racism. According to the test, whenever a character in the book was black, the person was referred to as "black," or a "negro," or a worse word, a word I, as a white person, could never say, and would never say, unlike almost all of the white people in *To Kill a Mockingbird*, who said that word all the time, even when they were alone and doing something random, like brushing their teeth; but whenever a character in the book was white, they were referred to not as "white" but rather as a "person." Was Atticus Finch's disinterest in challenging this rhetorical double standard not racist, somewhat racist, or definitely racist? the test had asked. You know what the right answer was, and so did I, and in that spirit, I should say that Mr. Crawford, and Ms. Hardaway, and the Instant Express deliveryman, and Mike were white, too. I didn't say that when they first appeared in this story because I hadn't taken the test yet.

Anyway, it was definitely Cheryl—a little older in the eyes and her black hair was gray-streaked but with that same big smile that showed plenty of gum. Her head filled the screen and other than that all I could see of her was that she'd wrapped a big, blue, shimmery scarf around her neck. I'd noticed this: So many women her age, our age, wore scarves, all the time, no matter the weather (it was summer where I was, and I assumed where she was, too), or the occasion (there was none, as far as I knew, unless I was considered an occasion). It was mysterious to me, and I'd tried to write a list—Three Reasons Why Middle-Aged Women Wear Scarves—as a way to try to understand the phenomenon, but so far I had only come up with one reason—that middle-aged women like their necks better when there are scarves around them—and as everyone knows you need at least three items to make a list. It's considered best practice in the list-making industry.

"You big a-hole," Cheryl said, and I remembered this, too: For Cheryl insults were endearments. "You haven't changed at all!" she said. I knew this wasn't true—I was bald, and I had a big, gray, bushy beard that suddenly I wanted to take off my face and put on my head—but I thanked her anyway, and then said the same thing about her, and she laughed and said, "Knucklehead, shut your mouth," and then we caught up. Or tried to. But our screens kept freezing. And then our dogs kept jumping into the picture—Cheryl had a dog, too, named Gracie—and then we spoke from the points of view of our dogs, in what we imagined would be their high, sweet human voices—"I like your scarf, Cheryl!"—and then our screens froze again and when they unfroze Cheryl said, "This is stupid. I wish we could just get together with the dogs or something." It turned out that we could—Cheryl lived close to me, a twenty minute walk away, just on the other side of Maude's favorite dog park—"I love that place!" said Gracie, through Cheryl. So we decided to meet there in an hour. But once we agreed on that, we didn't seem to want to get off the phone. We just sat there, grinning at each other. Until finally Cheryl said, "You know, I hadn't thought of that guy in years."

"What guy?" I said. Although of course I knew who she meant: Atticus Finch.

"But the minute I saw that link," Cheryl said, "I thought of you. You loved that book, and that guy. I don't think I ever met anyone who loved a character so much that he wanted to be him. You would walk around quoting him, just applying the things he said to random situations." Cheryl paused, unwrapped and wrapped her neck, then asked, "Do you remember that?

I didn't, not really, but even so I said, "Sure." Because my conversation with Ms. Hardaway had taught me even if I lied and told someone I remembered something they would tell me about it anyway, and in that way I would eventually remember.

"I guess it was cute," Cheryl said. "But I guess it was also annoying. For instance, when I was so upset because Therese Otto said I smelled like government cheese, you quoted, 'It's never an insult to be called what somebody thinks is a bad name. It just shows you how poor that person is, it doesn't hurt you.' And then, when Therese Otto apologized for saying I smelled like government cheese and when I told you it turned out that she was pretty nice after all, you quoted, 'Most people are, when you finally see them.' When we were in your rec room, watching a movie, which was *The Elephant Man*, and I said something basic, like, 'That guy grosses me out,' instead of saying something basic back in your own words, like, 'Yeah' or 'Me, too,' you quoted, 'You never really understand a person until you consider things from his point of view, until you climb into his skin and walk around in it.' The quoting, it was constant, Russell. And eventually, it drove me crazy. I'm sorry, but it did. I liked you, but even so I finally said, to myself, *If he quotes Atticus Finch one more time* . . . And then you did it." Cheryl drew a deep breath, and then continued. "We were sitting on a bench outside the cafeteria . . ." she said.

And then suddenly, I remembered. It was March, and cold. I hadn't yet cut off the sleeves of my sweatshirt. My arm was around Cheryl. I was so happy: because I had a girlfriend, and also because I'd just gotten an A on the test Mr. Crawford had given us to see if we'd read and understood *To Kill a Mockingbird*. "What about you?" I asked Cheryl, and she shrugged and my arm around her shoulders rose and fell.

"C+," she said, and then shrugged again. This surprised me. Cheryl was a better student than I was, and it was much more common for *her* to receive an A on a test, and *me* a C+.

"How come?" I said, because the test hadn't been hard—not for someone like me who loved the book and not even, I didn't think, for someone who didn't.

"I didn't read the whole thing," Cheryl said.

"You didn't read the whole test?"

"I didn't read the whole book."

"How much did you read?"

"Fifty pages," she said. "Maybe thirty."

"Shut up," I said. Because we'd talked about the book, constantly, over the past month—during study hall, when we were watching TV at my house or hers, when we were making out, or at least when we'd stopped making out to catch our breath and cool our jets, which is something that Cheryl had always said when our making out threatened to turn into something else. "Hey, loser, cool your jets," she'd say, and then, "What'd you think about chapter twelve in *To Kill a Mockingbird*?"

"*I* haven't been talking about it," Cheryl said. "You have. You quote lines from it all the time. Like, *all the time*. That's how I knew enough about it to get a C+."

"Why didn't you read the whole thing?"

"Because I didn't want to," Cheryl said.

"But it's a great book," I said, and Cheryl shrugged again.

"If you say so," she said. "Me, I didn't love it."

It was a line meant to end a conversation, and it did. I didn't know what Cheryl was feeling, but I felt used, and pissed off, too. How easy it is to hate the people who don't love what we love. That was my thought, now; my thought then was, *Fuck you*. I wanted to say it, too.

But I knew I shouldn't. Instead, I asked myself, as I often did, What would Atticus Finch say? Then, I mentally went through all the things that Atticus Finch had said in *To Kill a Mockingbird*, found the right one, took a deep breath, patted Cheryl's knee, and in a sage voice that didn't sound like mine, not even to me, I quoted, "Best way to clear the air is to have it all out in the open."

Cheryl nodded, like I'd confirmed something she already knew. Then, she took my hand off her knee, stood up, and said, "I'm breaking up with you, Russell. But don't worry. I bet you and Atticus will be very happy together."

"Fuck you," I said. It was a very un-Atticus-like thing for me to say, but that didn't seem to change Cheryl's mind about me. "Goodbye," she said. Then she walked away, and we'd not talked since, not once in thirty-seven years. And what was I supposed to say now? What do you say when the last words you said to a person you cared about were those words? *I'm sorry*, for starters. But would that be enough? Would it be a better apology if I told Cheryl that I was sorry *and* that I'd reckoned with Atticus Finch's racism? Probably. And I would have done that, but Cheryl was still talking on my phone screen and I didn't want to interrupt her.

"But maybe I was missing something. Maybe I've *been* missing something," Cheryl said. "Because do you know what I think now?" Then, Cheryl apparently told me what she thought now. That is, I saw her lips moving. But I couldn't hear what it was she was saying. I told her so, but now my screen had frozen, and so she couldn't hear me either. Although suddenly, I could hear her. She said "Hello, hello?" I said, "I'm here," but she still couldn't hear me. Cheryl muttered under her breath, then starting rubbing her eyes, just rubbing them and rubbing them. Finally, she stopped and I could see her eyes again. They looked tired, and I thought, God, we are so old, and we have wasted so much time. Although of course I didn't say that to Cheryl. Instead, I asked if she was OK. *This* she heard, and said, "Life hasn't worked out the way I wanted it to, Russell"

"Me neither," I said.

"I wanted to grow up to be a doctor who went wherever she was needed most. A doctor without borders," Cheryl said. "But instead, I became a life coach."

"That doesn't sound so bad," I said, although in truth, while I knew there were people who were life coaches, and while I had written a list called Nine Signs You Might Need a Life Coach, I had no idea what they did, or where they did it, if they coached from an office, or if they did it from home.

"Caring for yourself is an act of political warfare," Cheryl said.

"That's sounds like a quote," I said, and Cheryl nodded. "Audre Lorde said it." I nodded as though I knew exactly who Audre Lorde was, but Cheryl saw right through that. "Don't bullshit me, Russell. Audre Lorde. Poet. Black woman. For her taking care of herself probably *was* an act of political warfare. But I get paid to say it to people who have *always* done a pretty good job caring for themselves."

"White people," I guessed.

"White people," Cheryl agreed. She looked at me, head cocked, as though trying to make up her mind about me. Finally, she seemed to: She smiled widely again, and said, "Can I tell you something stupid? Atticus Finch meant so much to you that it made me jealous. I think that's why I broke up with you. Not because you were annoying. But because I was jealous." That *was* stupid, but sweet, like a lot of stupid things. But of course I didn't say that. Instead, I said something stupid myself: "*You* broke up with *me*? No, *I* broke up with *you*!" Cheryl laughed at that and said, "All right, you jerk, one hour, dog park, don't be late." Then she disappeared from my screen.

She disappeared from my screen, but still I kept staring at it, grinning at it. I thought about Cheryl, just twenty minutes away. I wondered if she was feeling what I was feeling: that something important was about to happen. I wondered if this was the way Mr. Crawford felt when he first taught *To Kill a Mockingbird*, or how Harper Lee felt when she first wrote *To Kill a Mockingbird*, or I felt when I first read *To Kill a Mockingbird* (I still didn't exactly remember), or how whoever wrote the article about white people needing to reckon with Atticus Finch's racism felt when they first wrote *that*.

Which reminded me that my T-shirt testifying that I had reckoned with Atticus Finch's racism was on its way. It was still a beautiful day outside, and so Maude and I went out on the porch. While I was out there, I read two alerts on my phone: one, an automatic alert, telling me it was time to order new contact lenses (and I did that), and two, an active shooter alert. But before I could read more about the active shooter, the Instant Express Delivery van pulled up in front of my house. The same driver as before hopped out of the van, and said, "Here you go!" He handed me a padded envelope, tossed Maude a treat, and then sped off to his next house to deliver his next package.

I opened the envelope and there it was: a black T-shirt that said in white letters I Reckoned with Atticus Finch's Racism. I immediately took off the T-shirt I'd been wearing—that T-shirt had words on it, too, but the second I took it off I forgot what they were—and put on the new one, and felt that heart-singing feeling you get when you receive a good report card. In this case the report card was the T-shirt, which fit me, too, much better than the old one. It fit me so well, that I closed my eyes and tried to picture Cheryl, what she would think when she saw me walking up to her at the dog park wearing this T-shirt. There, in my mind's eye, was Cheryl, in her scarf and with her dog. She saw me and waved, and smiled, and I saw those gums, and I was so happy, and she seemed so happy, too. But then she squinted, and cocked her head. Cheryl was looking at my T-shirt. But she wasn't seeing how well it fit me. She was seeing . . . well, I didn't know. Was she was seeing a guy who was mature enough, thoughtful enough, evolved enough, to renounce a book, even though that book had meant so much to him as a boy? Or was she seeing a man who had rejected—or even worse, basically forgotten—something fundamental to him, a man whose most cherished things were so meaningless to him that he could just take them on and off like a T-shirt, a man who had changed so much that she didn't know him anymore and didn't want to know him anymore?

And then I thought: Uh-oh, here it comes again: another reckoning. Life, I was learning, was full of them, and just because you've successfully reckoned with something and gotten a T-shirt to commemorate your accomplishment doesn't mean your work is done, and it doesn't mean the next reckoning will be as easily pulled off as the previous one. And even if you do pull it off, you might not get a T-shirt for your efforts. But that was fine. I was willing to reckon with the T-shirt, just as I'd reckoned with Atticus Finch's racism, if that's what Cheryl wanted me to do. Whatever Cheryl wanted me to reckon with, I would do that. Because—and this was another reckoning—except for my dog and my phone, I'd been alone, for so long. And I didn't want to be alone anymore.

"Russell," I heard someone say. I opened my eyes and there, standing in front of me was Mike. No Legend, just Mike. He was still holding the gun in his right hand. Earlier, he'd held it up, chest level, so that anyone could see it. Now, it dangled at his side. Not like he was hiding it, but like he'd forgotten it was there. There was something wrong with his eyes, too. They seemed like he was looking at something far away. Maude growled at him, deep in her throat, which I thought was strange—she'd never growled at him before. But then, she'd never seen him without Legend before, either.

"Mike, where's Legend?" I asked him.

"He ran away when I fired the gun," Mike said, and his voice was far away, too. Although suddenly his eyes came into focus, and stared directly at my chest. And by my chest, I mean my T-shirt.

"Fired the gun?" I asked, and Mike told me who he'd fired at, who he'd shot and killed, and why. The entire time he kept staring at my T-shirt.

"Atticus *Finch*," I said, when he was finished with his story. I pointed at my T-shirt. "He wasn't a person who shot a dog in real life. He was a character. In a novel. *To Kill a Mockingbird*."

"I remember now," Mike said. "I really liked that book back in middle school."

And then he shot Maude, and she died. And then he shot me, and I died.

And then I had a vision. In it I was standing in front of my old middle school, which, as Ms. Hardaway had said, had been right across the street front my old high school. The high school was gone. In its place was a parking lot. There was a pedestrian bridge arching over the road to connect the lot to the middle school. There were no cars in the lot, which was instead full of people. A line of people that coiled and snaked through the parking lot, out of the parking lot, onto the ground on one side of the bridge, and then back on the other side, and then up the stairs that led up to the bridge and into the middle school. The line looked like it was moving slowly. The people in line in the parking lot looked relatively healthy, but the people on the bridge looked very sick: They were stooped over, and some of them were crying, or gasping, or both. At the edge of the parking lot were two women, in nursing uniforms. When I saw them I understood that the middle school had been turned into a hospital. One of the nurses was handing out umbrellas to people who were about to cross under the bridge; the other was collecting umbrellas from people who were about to start climbing the stairs to the bridge. I wondered what the umbrellas were for, but just then one person on the bridge leaned over the railing and vomited, onto the umbrellas of the people underneath. Then another person vomited, which then led to another person vomiting, and then the entire bridge seemed to be vomiting onto the umbrellas held by the people below.

I wasn't sure what any of this had to do with me until I saw an old, hunched-over bald man fold up his umbrella and hand it to one of the nurses. It was my eighth-grade English teacher, Mr. Crawford. He was wearing the clothes he'd always worn in class. They'd looked shabby thirty-seven years ago; they looked worse now. So did Mr. Crawford. His skin was papery, his lips translucent. He was about to start climbing the stairs, but when I said his name he paused and looked at me, in silence. His tongue darted in and out of his mouth, then rooted around for something in his teeth. "Johnson, what in the world are you wearing?" he finally asked. I told him. Mr. Crawford opened his mouth to say something in response but then started coughing, hard, and didn't seem to be able to stop. I wondered if he was going to start vomiting right there, before he even made it to the bridge, but he managed to stop coughing before it came to that. He started walking up the stairs and I walked with him. When we got to the top of stairs, Mr. Crawford said, "Well, what's brought you here, Johnson? Make it quick. I don't have much time before I go . . ." And here he pointed toward the other end of the bridge, where people were entering the hospital.

I told him, about the link, and about how it had caused me to call him, and then how Ms. Hardaway had called me, and then Cheryl, and about how I'd taken the test and gotten this T-shirt, and then how Mike had shot Maude, and then me. Mr. Crawford closed his eyes as I talked, and they stayed closed for some time afterward. Finally, he opened his eyes. They looked filmy, as though there was something between them and me.

"I'm sorry to hear that things didn't work out with Watterson," he said. "I'd always dreamed of a future for the two of you. Full of children. Rewarding jobs. Overflowing bookshelves. Inventive sexual lives. With occasional insatiable exhibitionist needs. I'm speaking, of course, of intercourse in public. Grocery store bathrooms. Back rows of planetariums." Mr. Crawford closed his eyes again. "That booth at Arby's. No, not that booth, the other one."

"Really?" I said, and Mr. Crawford opened his eyes.

"Really, Johnson. Students always think their teachers are creepy, but they have no idea. But let's not talk about that. You want me to tell you whether or not Atticus Finch is racist. Am I correct?" I thought about this, thought about another reason why I would be having this vision. I couldn't think of one. Yes, I told Mr. Crawford, that's what I want you to tell me. "Why?" he asked. "Suppose I say *Yes*? Will that make you feel better? Suppose I say *No*? Will that make you feel worse?" He paused to let me answer. But I didn't. I felt like I was back in middle school, when Mr. Crawford tended to ask me questions that only he had the answers to. "Why ask me in the first place?" he continued. "I remember you being an enthusiastic reader. Dense, but dogged. In the B+ range. Why don't you just reread the book?" Again, he paused to let me answer, and again, I didn't, and again, Mr. Crawford continued. "What happens to us, Johnson, when we get older? We're supposed to get wiser. But I think we only get scared. And lazy. And then we forget, because we're too scared and lazy to remember. And because we're old." He raised his index finger, as though telling me to wait a minute, and then vomited over the railing. When he was done, he wiped his mouth with his jacket sleeve, turned back to me. "Fine," he said, in a croaking voice. "I'll tell you. But before I do, you need to answer one question for me." We'd been shuffling forward all this time, and we were almost at the door to the hospital by now. "Johnson," Mr. Crawford asked, "what's it like to be dead?" And finally, I knew the answer to one of Mr. Crawford's questions.

"It's like taking a long walk without your dog," I said, and then suddenly I was back at my house. Maude wasn't waiting for me, but there was a package, sitting on my front porch. I took it inside. Flicked on the lights, or tried to, but the power was out. It was very dark, very quiet inside the house. There was nothing in there except for me, and the pile of packages, and my new package. I couldn't even remember what was in it, what I might have ordered. I threw the package on top of the pile. Then I picked it up, and threw it at the pile, as hard as I could, and then again, and again, and again. I threw it for hours, until the sun came up and there was light in the hallway and finally the package burst open. In it were the contact lenses I'd ordered, little fake eyes in little plastic pouches, scattered all over the floor.

BIG VELCRO

My husband wanted to go a minor league hockey game.

You mean, before you die? I asked.

No, he said, tonight, there's a game tonight, I want to go to a minor league hockey game tonight.

It seemed a dumb thing to want to do. But in our marriage vows we had sworn that we would never force our own idea of happiness on each other, and so I said, Sure, OK, go ahead, if that's what you want to do, it's fine with me, I support you.

No, he said, I want *us* to go to a minor league hockey game. Together.

Oh, I said. My husband had a hopeful look on his face that made me want to hurt him, and so I looked away from him, and at the ceiling, which is what I do when I pretend to be thinking hard about something. There was a blurry, amorphous stain up there that made me think of a country whose borders are constantly being disputed. What are the teams? I pretended to want to know. He told me. The names of the teams made reference to each city's former primary industry, but in a way that was supposed to make the failure of that city's industry sound whimsical and not depressing. For instance, our city was the center of the region's once-thriving but now defunct gravel industry, and we were the Rock Dragons. I don't remember what the other team's name was. The Tool and Die Tornados. The Flour City Fury. Something of that nature. Oh, I said, again, and my husband asked that I stop saying that.

Say something else, he said.

I'm pregnant, I said.

Are you sure? my husband said, and I nodded, still staring at the ceiling, and, quoting my gynecologist, said, No method of birth control is one hundred percent effective, and then, also quoting my gynecologist, added, Yes, even thirty-eight-year-old women get pregnant when they don't want to.

Oh, my husband said, and I looked away from the ceiling and at him, expecting him to be looking at the ceiling, which I knew was the thing he did when he actually *was* thinking hard about something. But no, he was looking at me, with that same hopeful look on his face, and it didn't make me want to hurt him anymore, but it did make me want to be somewhere far away. I named a place.

I've already been there, my husband said.

You have? I said. I found this shocking. Because we had reached the point in our life together where I'd just assumed everything was known.

Yeah, he said, I was there for two weeks in the early aughts, protesting Big Velcro.

When my husband said that, I realized that I *had* known that he'd been to that place, doing that thing, and that I'd willed myself to forget it, which was what I had to do whenever my husband talked about his time as an activist protesting the unfair labor practices and environmental atrocities perpetrated by the seven major international Velcro manufacturers who together made up the thing my husband and possibly no one else referred to as "Big Velcro." Yes, I'd willed myself to forget this, which was what I had to do to make sure my marriage survived my husband telling stories about how he'd protested Big Velcro, the way that Big Velcro itself had survived my husband protesting it.

Never mind. I named another place.

That place? Why? my husband wanted to know.

Because it seems like a good place to have a baby, I answered. I don't know why I said that, because no place seemed like an especially good place to have a baby. Yes, it seems like as good a place as any to have a baby, I said anyway.

Well, it's not, my husband said.

How do you know? I almost asked him, but I knew that if I did, he would tell me that he'd protested Big Velcro there, too, and so I said, Fine, you name a place. He did. No way, I said, that's an awful place to raise a baby.

How do you know? he asked.

I've already been there, I said. He seemed shocked to learn this, and I could tell that he'd assumed he'd known everything about me, too.

"Really? he said.

Yes, I said, I was there for two weeks, in the early aughts.

Doing what? my husband wanted to know. In truth, I'd been there for only three days, on a post-college-graduation trip with my best friend, seeing the world, or at least parts of it, and I'd said I'd been there for two weeks instead of three days because it sounded better, the way saying I was pregnant sounded better than just saying, Oh, although I was in fact pregnant, whereas I really had only spent three days and not two weeks in that place would be an awful place to raise a baby. But instead of saying all that, I said I was there protesting Big Velcro.

Very funny, my husband said, and then he added, much more earnestly, You know, I think that's the first time you've ever even said the words Big Velcro, and I said I'm sure that's not true, and he said that he was sure that it was, and so I said, several more times, Big Velcro, Big Velcro, Big Velcro, Big Velcro, and then he said, still very earnestly, There's nothing funny about Big Velcro, and then I said, You know, Big Velcro would make a good name for a minor league hockey team.

Oh, you think you're so smart, my husband said. And I did not like the way he said that, I did not like it at all. In fact, it reminded me of why I didn't like the place I'd just told my husband I'd spent two weeks in in the early aughts. I remembered it well. The swaying palm trees lining the streets, which should have been very pretty except for all the paper cups, the plastic bags, the diapers scattered around them. The animals—pigs, sheep, goats, dogs, cats—constantly being herded, or wandering, into traffic, where they were hit, or not, it didn't seem to matter to anyone, not even the animals. But mostly I remembered the women: There weren't any. Only men: men walking on the sidewalk, men in the middle of the street, men driving cars, men sitting at cafes, facing not each other but the street. One day I walked past one of those cafes, which was next to a mosque and was called Snack Islam. At Snack Islam were several youngish men wearing clothes that resembled my future husband's clothes: jeans, sweaters, sneakers. And there were also several older men, and most of these were wearing brown, pointy-hooded, full-length robes that appeared to be made of burlap. They all watched me as I walked by, and the looks on their faces—aggrieved, threatened—resembled the look on my husband's face when he said, Oh you think you're so smart, and so I know they were saying the same thing to me, with their faces, and minds, and one of the things that made me so smart, apparently, was that I had the nerve as a woman to walk down the street in the middle of the day, and I had two not-unrelated thoughts, which were that there were too many men in the world, and also that every good thing in that world was turning to shit. Those thoughts made me feel like crying, and I didn't want those men to see me cry, so I turned away from them and toward the street in front of me, and saw a sign with a picture of several pigs crossing a road. Underneath the sign, several sheep were crossing the road. Behind them a boy clapped his hands until all the sheep had made it to the other side and then begun eating the garbage underneath the palm trees.

And then I did start crying—not just in the place that would be an awful place to raise our child, but also right after telling the story about why it would be an awful place to raise our child. My husband didn't say anything. He didn't look aggrieved or threatened anymore. Now he looked sheepish, his eyes lowered, his chin tucked into his chest. I was glad. His sheepishness was exactly what I hoped would come out of the story. What a gratifying thing, I thought, when a story has such a direct and immediate effect. No wonder people tell so many of them.

Are you done? my husband asked. I thought he meant was I done crying. It seemed kind of a callous question and made me want to tell my story again, but maybe weaponize it with even more feeling and righteousness this time. Although in fact I was done crying. This seemed obvious, so I didn't bother to answer his question. Very funny, he said, again, and again in a way that made it clear it wasn't, and I wonder if anyone in the history of phrasemaking has ever used that one without meaning its opposite.

Clarify, I said.

That was *my* story, he said.

The possessiveness of the beloved! We'd had this same argument over food, books, cars, LPs, CDs, DVDs, pets, pens, kitchen utensils, travel mugs, phones, cameras, snow shovels, sweaters, pillows, current friends who also, strangely, often, then became former friends. I wondered if the same thing would happen with our child. It wasn't your story, I said, knowing he would say it was, and also knowing that his story would have something to do with Big Velcro.

It was, he said. *I* was there, in 2004, protesting Big Velcro. I told you about it. Remember? Big Velcro was planning to build a new factory in the city's untaxed, unregulated international industrial zone. No environmental regulations. No tax money going to the local people. No promises that the local people would get the jobs. And then we stopped them! They didn't end up building a factory there after all! We actually did it! I told you all about it. Remember?

I didn't remember, because of course I never really listened to his stories about Big Velcro. But I didn't say that. Nor did I wonder, out loud, whether the local people might not have been entirely happy that a factory where at least some of them might have ended up getting jobs didn't open because of protests by people who were not local and who then left that place after making sure the factory didn't open there. I didn't say either of these things. I just want some credit for that. Why is it that we don't ever get credit for the things we *don't* say? For the first time, I felt something like my husband's nuttiness for reforming Big Velcro. How could I change the world so that by the time my child was born into it it would be a place where people got credit for the things they *didn't* say?

Yeah, my husband said. I told you all about it. Not just the protest, but what I saw on the way to and from the industrial zone. The animals. The palm trees. The garbage. The guys. My husband sat back in his chair—we were sitting at opposite ends of our kitchen table, which is where we seemed to have most of our arguments, as though our arguments were meals, although in fact we tended to eat in the TV room, plates on our laps—crossed his arms over his chest, which must be a survival technique among the smugly self-assured, and said, I *know* you remember this.

You know I don't listen to your stories about Big Velcro, I said, finally, after years of wanting to say it. I saw from the ruined look on his face that the remark had landed, too, like a punch. My husband opened his mouth, ready to say more, but I didn't stick around to hear it. Instead, I walked into the TV room and called Liz, who lived the next state over. Liz! College roommate, forever best friend, platonic soulmate, reliable reassurer, trusted sharer of the heart's secrets and longings! We'd lived together for four years, traveled to parts of the world together for four months, and since then we'd been promising and failing to visit each other for sixteen years. She picked up the phone and didn't interrupt and just listened as I told her everything. This was her job, as my friend: to listen to my story and then, at the end of it, tell me the thing I needed to hear, which was the thing I wanted to hear, which was, in this case, that my story was mine and not my husband's. Liz had always been excellent at her job, too—that is, at her job as a friend, and, by extension, I assumed, at her real job, which was as a child psychologist. I thought I'd certainly send my child to her, when the time came for it to need a child psychologist, which it certainly would.

You expected hugs from the natives, Liz said, when she was done listening. The hostility in her voice was unignorable, and once again I wondered if every good thing in the world was going to shit.

I didn't expect hugs from anyone.

You expected opulence.

I don't know what I expected.

You expected there to be villas. And in one of those villas you expected to be reclining on enormous cushions while someone dusky fed you dates.

I didn't expect that. But it's true that I didn't expect it to be so seedy, I admitted.

It's the second world, she said.

I thought it was the third world.

It's the second world, Liz said, and then named another place, a place she and I had also visited, which she said was the third world. The third world is dangerous, she said.

I didn't say the place was dangerous. I said it was seedy.

That's because that place is in the second world. The second world is seedy. The third world is dangerous. Jesus, everyone knows that.

Are you mad at me? I asked her.

Yes, she said.

I paused to consider why. What I had done to Liz recently? Nothing, that I could think of. But then again, I couldn't think of anything I'd done *for* her recently, either.

I'm sorry, I said, which I hoped would pretty much cover it.

There are no other women, Liz said.

In your life? I said.

In your story, Liz said.

Yes, that's right, I said. It was a lonely feeling.

Liz sighed. I knew that sigh. It was the noise she made when she couldn't believe she was going to have to slowly lead me to the answer that should have been obvious to anyone, even my unborn child, who I made a mental note to tell Liz about just as soon she was done leading me to the obvious answer. Why are you calling me? she asked.

To confirm that yes, the story I told my husband was my story, not his.

And why are you asking *me* to do that?

Because you were with me, I said.

Correct, Liz said. She paused, I suppose to let this sink in, but there must be something nonporous in me. Yes, I was a blacktop driveway of a friend, a human, and no doubt, thinking into the future, a mother. Nothing ever sunk in. Liz sighed again. I was with you in real life, she said, but in your story you say you were the only woman in that place. So which is it? Was I there, or wasn't I there?

Both, I wanted to say, but didn't. Because I kind of remembered this about Liz now: She had always been a little *sensitive*. And one of the things she was a little *sensitive* about was that I was so selfish and took her for granted, that as a friend I *took*, but I never *gave*. I'm not your friend, she once said to me, and in fact had said this more than once, and in fact had said this more than once during our four-month trip around the world, and in fact, I was pretty sure she'd said it to me in that place about which I'd told a story that my husband insisted was his.

You *are* my friend, I'd said back to her, those many times.

I'm not, she'd insisted.

Then what are you? I'd wanted to know.

I'm like a giant *ear* that you just keep around so you have something to complain into, she'd complained.

God, Liz could be touchy. I was remembering that now, which was maybe why we hadn't seen each other in sixteen years, and also why it had been sometimes difficult to travel with her. Which was maybe why I'd sometimes left the hotel while she was in the bathroom, without telling her, so I could walk the city alone. I'd apologized for doing this at the time, I remembered that now too, after I got back to the hotel and complained about the men and the animals and she complained about being a giant ear. Well, I wasn't going to apologize again. Not because I wasn't sorry, but because you can only say sorry so many times before even people who feel like believing you stop believing you.

I'm pregnant, I said instead.

Oh, Liz said.

Oh? I said.

Should I have said something different? Liz said.

Like congratulations? I suggested.

God, what do you *want*? Liz said, and then she hung up.

Well! It's not often that someone asks you a question worth answering. I sat down on the couch to think of how I might do that, and as I did I happened to look out the bay window, and through the window I saw my husband, pants down by his ankles, taking a shit right on the driveway.

Oh my god! I said, and ran outside. Although I didn't run directly outside. First I had to put on my shoes, because it was cold out, snow on the ground, and in fact on the driveway my husband was just shitting on. Then, shoes on, my hand on the front-door knob, I remembered that I'd left my phone on the couch, and though I didn't know why I'd want or need the phone, it was often the case that you only discovered that you wanted or needed your phone when you didn't have it. So I went to the couch and dug around the cushions. I pocketed the phone, then finally left the house, and found that my husband was not anywhere to be seen, nor our car, but there was the pile of shit, looking black and dense and so hot it was steaming, an actual, steaming pile of shit on our unshoveled snow-covered driveway. I stood over it, considered it as a detective would a clue, and a minute later our neighbor, a bald, gray-bearded man named John, joined me. He didn't say anything for a while, just stood there scratching his beard, thoughtfully, as though this were one of life's mysteries and we should take our time contemplating it. I didn't know John well, but at this point I was happy for his company and had nothing against him.

It's not mine, I finally said, about the shit, just to get that out of the way.

John nodded. We watched the shit steam less and less and then stop altogether, and then John said, I've noticed that you don't really shovel your driveway.

What?

I said I've noticed that you don't really shovel your driveway.

I heard what you said, I said.

Then why did you say *what*? John wanted to know.

Because I was confused, I said.

Why do people say *what* when they mean *why* or *when* or *how*? John asked, sounding suddenly not like whatever kind of professional he was, but instead like the community-college lecturer in writing and rhetoric and public speaking that I was.

That's an excellent question, I said.

Thank you, John said.

Meanwhile, I said, and gestured toward my husband's pile of shit, which was easily the most interesting thing he'd ever made, or done (he was also now a lecturer, in industrial relations, at the community college). Yes, it was definitely first place, had won the blue ribbon, and

I thought what a great thing it would be to actually have a blue ribbon to place on my husband's pile of shit. Though on second thought maybe John could do the placing, since he was wearing gloves and I wasn't.

My husband did this, I said, to John, still gesturing at the shit. He continued to nod and scratch his beard, and then he said, Because once you drive over the snow it's pretty much impossible to shovel off, and then it's just a mess for the rest of the winter.

I confess that even I, a lecturer in writing and rhetoric and public speaking at the community college, didn't know what to say to this. I pointed at my husband's now-cold-but-still-mysterious deposit, the best and most miraculous thing he had ever made, definitely better and more miraculous than helping make our baby, which frankly pretty much anyone could do and pretty much anyone has done. Whereas shitting on your own driveway was something pretty much anyone could do, except, in my experience, to my knowledge, no one ever did except for my husband. This, I wanted to say, *this* is what we should be talking about.

But somehow, when it came time for me to speak, it was as though the words were John's or at least the subject was, and I was now speaking his concerns and not mine. We don't have to shovel it if we don't want, I said. It's *our* driveway.

For the first time since we'd gotten together to stand over my husband's shit, John seemed surprised. I knew this because he finally stopped scratching his beard and nodding. These things matter, he said. At least, they matter to us.

Which—These things matter—was exactly what my husband had always said about protesting Big Velcro, and in fact his voice, when he said that, sounded like John's when he discovered that I didn't feel as he did about driveway clearance: surprised, and a little superior, and a lot hurt. Which had always made me want to hurt my husband, and now it made me want to hurt John, too. I just had one question before I tried to do that.

Us? I said, because we'd lived in our house for seven years, and in all that time I was pretty sure I'd only ever seen John.

Yes, John said. Us. Me and John.

Oh my god, I said. I thought *your* name was John.

It is, he said, in that same surprised, hurt, superior way, and then he went back inside his house.

And how had we gotten here? This was something I asked my students when one of their speeches went off track, which they inevitably did. So, moving backward, there was John, who apparently lived with another John, and my husband shitting on the driveway, and there was that upsetting conversation with Liz, and before that there was that upsetting conversation with my husband, and before that there was Big Velcro, and all during this time I was pregnant, and at the very beginning my husband wanted to go to the minor league hockey game, and I assumed that's where he was right now.

I started walking toward the Civic Center. The streets were empty, as seemed appropriate for the center of the region's once thriving but now defunct gravel industry. The houses needed painting if they hadn't already been covered with vinyl siding, and if they had then the siding needed washing. I noticed that most of the driveways hadn't been shoveled, and most of the driveways that hadn't been shoveled had been driven on and were messy with crusted-over tracks. The miracle of my husband's shit seemed like it had happened a long time ago. I felt tired, and my thoughts wandered, as they tend to when I'm tired, until they landed on Liz's question: What did I want? I didn't know, and it seemed that I had never known, but I did know what I didn't want: I didn't want to have a baby—not there, not anywhere, not with anyone, and certainly not with my husband, because I didn't really love him, didn't even really care enough to hate him the way he'd hated Big Velcro, and of course I didn't care about going to see the Rock Dragons play, either, and only went inside the Civic Center to tell my husband all these things before I left him.

It seemed like the entire city was inside the Civic Center, every single citizen yelling and striking the Plexiglas with open hands and screaming at team employees wearing khaki pants to fire T-shirts at them out of their T-shirt cannons. Then there was the game itself, the sounds of blades scraping the ice and sticks slapping against sticks and once in a while fists against faces and helmets. I was entranced, I was mesmerized, and in that state I wandered the place, looking for my husband, but I couldn't find him, so I took the phone out of my pocket and texted him, and when he didn't text back I called him.

We live next to two Johns, I said when he picked up.

I know, my husband said. His voice sounded dead, exactly the opposite of how it sounded when he talked about his fight against Big Velcro.

Who is the other John? I said, and I could hear my husband sigh, and I realized that this—the identity of the other John—was something I should have known, something my husband had probably talked about, many times, and I would have known about the other John had I listened, had I paid attention to the world around me.

His differently abled son, my husband said, and it's true, that's something you'd think I would have known.

How differently abled is he? I said, and I don't know why I said that.

Mildly.

Oh good, I said, and I didn't know why I said that, either. Where are you?

At the airport, my husband said.

Oh, I said, for the last time in this story. Because I knew what being at the airport meant: It meant that he was leaving me before I left him. And it also meant that he wasn't in the Civic Center, and so I no longer had any reason to be there, either. I left the building and began to walk home, my phone still pressed against my ear. Where are you going? I asked, and he told me: It was someplace far away, someplace I'd never been, and I didn't need to ask what he'd be protesting there.

It really was my story, my husband said.

I don't really love you, I said back, because that was the truth, and there was no reason not to tell it anymore.

I know, he said, and his voice sounded so tired, because he knew it, and must have known it for a long time.

And I'm not really pregnant, I said, even though that was not the truth, because I knew it would make it easier for him to leave me, completely, and forever—not that I wanted to make things easier for him, but I did want him gone.

I didn't *think* so, he said, suddenly sounding a lot less tired. God, he said, really fired up now, God, you're a selfish asshole.

Goodbye, I said, and then hung up. As I walked I thought vaguely hopeful thoughts about my future—sure, my husband would no longer be in it, and maybe Liz wouldn't either, but that was OK, because things hadn't been so fantastic with them in my life anyway, and besides, I'd have a baby (I hadn't wanted the baby, but that did not mean I wasn't going to have the baby), and we'd make a life together, a life in which I'd be a happier, more generous, less selfish person—until I got to my house. There, in front of me, was our driveway. It had been shoveled, and my husband's shit was gone, and even though I knew this was all for the best, still, I was so fucking sad.

THE BIG BOOK OF USELESS SATURDAYS

1)

I am watching a football game, on television. It's snowing there, where the game is being played. It's also snowing where I live. I mean, not in my living room, but outside. I can see the flakes through the window, which is just to the left of the television set.

"Hey, look," I say to my son as he walks into the room. I point at the television. "It's snowing there, too."

He smiles. I know that smile. It's the smile he smiles right before he says that I must be joking.

"You must be joking," he says. He pauses to see if I am, but once again, no. "There," he says, "is here." He points at the television, and then he points out the window. I look at the television, then at the window, then at the television, until I finally understand his meaning: The game on television is being played in the same city where we live. And I knew this. The game is sold out. That's why I am watching it on television. I'm even wearing the team's jersey, a fifty-year-old man wearing a football jersey, a little tighter than it was the previous year.

"There is something wrong with me," I say, to my son, but he isn't in the room with me anymore. A second later, I see him, through the window, throwing a football to himself in the snow.

2)

"There is something wrong with me," said my mother. We were in the waiting room in her doctor's office. At the opposite end of the waiting room was a very large, rectangular fish tank, gurgling. There was only one fish inside. We were the only people in the waiting room, even though, relatively speaking, the waiting room was as big as the fish tank. It looked as though someone had anticipated a lot more fish, and sick people.

"You're an old woman. Of course there's something wrong with you" is what I didn't say.

"I'm not ready for you to die" is what I didn't say, either.

"Let's just see what the doctor has to say" is what I said instead.

3)

My father was himself a doctor, a world-famous oncologist, who devised the radical treatment—"The Radical," so called—that while not exactly curing cancer made it so that most people who had the disease could live with it for a long time. After he retired he traveled all over the world, giving talks—always on a Saturday—about The Radical, talks about how he had done what he had done, and how he hoped it would it would inspire other people to do other great things, too. After a few years of this he died, on Grand Cayman Island, of gout, but before he did he gave talks at convention centers, memorial halls, hospital operating theaters, colleges, universities, but mostly at all-inclusive golf resorts.

He asked my mother to come along with him on these trips, because he was afraid he'd be bored and lonely, and my mother did, and found *herself* bored and lonely, and so she wrote a memoir, also world-famous, about that experience, called *The Big Book of Useless Saturdays*.

4)

This was the first sentence in my mother's world-famous memoir: "At the Aloha Ridge Grand West Wind, my husband is everything, and I am nothing, and both the chicken and the shrimp are coconut encrusted."

5)

Outside the snow has gotten thicker, and through it I can barely see my son now playing football with the neighborhood kids, seven of them, all girls. My son is quarterback. Lined up across from him is the nose tackle, I guess is what you'd call her position. She's crouched down and her fingers are twitching like she can't hardly wait to knock the *shit* out of him.

6)

There are things buried in the yard. One Christmas we'd had lobster and trash pickup wasn't due for another week, and I didn't want the shells stinking up the garbage bin and so I buried the shells underneath the red maple. Also, we'd had a dog, Pepper, sweet thing, she'd had a heart attack, and we buried her in the southeast corner. And then there's a gun, a Walther. I've buried and reburied that one so many times that I've almost forgotten where I buried it the last time.

7)

"If you dig up that gun one more time . . ." my wife said, but I'd already had the shovel in hand, and she never did bother to finish the sentence.

8)

"All the sentences no one is interested in hearing me finish could make up a whole other book," wrote my mother in *The Big Book of Useless Saturdays*.

9)

My mother got up and walked across the waiting room. She had a few things she wanted to say to the receptionist about how long she'd been kept waiting already, and how much longer she could expect to be kept waiting after she'd said the things she wanted to say. I watched my mother go—my mother, so full of life and rage in her world-famous memoir, now so diminished and enfeebled that she had to pause and rest, three times, on her journey from one end of the waiting room to the other. The receptionist, a woman half my mother's age, which is to say, my age, sat behind her high counter—from my vantage point just a head—regarding my mother with a barely patient expression on her face that made me want to shoot her with the Walther, except that I didn't know that there was such a gun as the Walther yet, let alone that my mother would ask me to shoot her with it, let alone that I would bury it and rebury it several times in my backyard.

My phone rang in my pocket. I took it out, and in answering it, turned away from my mother and toward the fish tank. The fish, bright, flashing blue, was nosing around a gray plastic treasure chest with its lid half open.

"Any news?" my wife asked on the phone.

I told her that we hadn't even seen the doctor yet, that we were still in the waiting room. "What's our son up to?" I asked.

"He and the neighborhood girls are in the backyard."

"Playing football?"

"Being interviewed by channel eight about playing football." My wife described the scene as seen by her through our living room window: a fat middle-aged man with a camera on his shoulder and a slender middle-aged woman holding a microphone. This was the fourth time a local news channel had done something about the football being played in our backyard. One boy and seven girls, playing backyard football. There was something to be made of this, although no one seemed exactly clear what. "Who is the woman with the microphone talking to?" I asked, although I already knew who.

"Our son. As always."

Just then, I heard my mother raise her voice. It sounded like the complaint of a piece of dry, splintering wood being stepped on. "I have to go," I told my wife, hung up, and turned back to the receptionist's counter.

"But I'm the only person here," my mother said.

"What a strange thing to say," the receptionist said. "Of course you're not the only person here."

10)

In chapter two of *The Big Book of Useless Saturdays*, my father told an overflow crowd at the annual gathering of American pediatric oncologists in Ballroom A of the Tobagoan Regency Colonial, "The fight against cancer can feel lonely. But I am here to tell you that you are not alone," while my mother was in their room, alone, in bed at three in the afternoon, drinking her third whatsitcalled of the day, watching my father speak on the resort's closed circuit television channel.

11)

It's halftime on the game on television. I look out the window. My son is lying, back-down, in the snow, covered by snow. I wonder how long he's been lying there. One of the girls is standing over him, with her right arm extended, hand open. My son sticks out his arm, grabs her hand, and she pulls him to his feet. On the ground is the outline of my son's body, dead brown grass surrounded by snow.

Suddenly, all eight kids' heads turn toward the street, and there, trotting toward them, toward the backyard, is a fat middle-aged man with a large camera on his shoulder and a slender middle-aged woman holding a microphone. Behind them, on the street, the white Channel 4 Action News Team van, still running. I can see the exhaust, gray puffs out of the tailpipe and into the snowy air.

12)

"I think we should clear the air," I said to my wife, once I'd come in from reburying the Walther. It was three in the morning but she looked like she was going to the gym—black spandex shorts and a red tank top and her hair pulled back into a ponytail and a backpack hooked over her shoulders. I was standing at the bottom of the stairs, she halfway up, hands on the railing, looking down on me like someone about to sing a wistful song in a musical.

"Do you love me?" my wife said.

"I do."

"Then you'll stop burying and reburying the Walther?"

"I can't."

"OK," she said. "I'm going to leave you now." And there, just like that, the air was cleared. There was just one more thing left in it.

"What about our son?" I said.

"He can decide for himself whether he wants to stay or go," my wife said. But she said this sadly, and without much hope. After all, why would he want to go somewhere else? Here, he had everything he wanted: his football, the backyard, the neighborhood girls. The news teams knew exactly where to find him.

13)

From chapter five of *The Big Book of Useless Saturdays*:

"I couldn't find you," my husband says to me. This is at the Monterey Cedar Dunes and Spa. I am sitting under a cedar tree, one of many lining the fairway, dogleg left, leading up to the eleventh green at the Monterey Cedar Dunes, which, on the backside sloped downward, toward the cliff, and then the rocks, and then the blue flashing water, a beautiful spot that nonetheless is the ruin of many a mood, an afternoon, a scorecard, a handicap.

"You look young when you look confused. I like you so much better when you look confused than I do when you're in front of an audience, when you're an authority, an old man who is an expert in his field who eats so much it'll be the death of him" is what I want to say to him. "Where did you look?" I say instead.

He lists the usual places where he looks for me after one of his talks: the spa, the pool, the beach, the pilates class, the shuffleboard court, the bar, the other bar, the room.

"Well, I was here," I say, and then I write those words down in my notebook, which is on my lap and which my husband notices for the first time, and when he does, he looks even more confused, lost even, and for the first time in a long time I feel like I might love him, still, again, although not enough to put away the notebook.

"What are you doing?" he wants to know.

I tell him.

"Why?"

"Because I'm bored and I want to see if I can turn boredom into a book, the way you turned cancer into a disease that kills you later rather than sooner" is what I want to say.

"Because I want to be useful," I say instead.

14)

"Can I help?" I asked my mother, and the doctor's receptionist.

"I was there to interview Donaldson," the receptionist said to my mother, in a bright, warbly voice. Up close she looked older than she had from across the room, much closer to my mother's age than mine. She was wearing a very long, very wide, shiny, expensive looking blood-colored scarf, the kind that suggested she was an artist, or a patron of one. "Tall. Stooped. Bird-faced. Like nothing so much as a vulture, an omniscient one. And handsome, yes. Although of course there was nothing between us. Although on the other hand of course there was. After all, he was Donaldson."

Here she paused. I assumed she expected my mother to say something, but my mother just stared at her, dead-eyed, her mouth screwed up tight. I recognized the look: It was the look my mother always gave someone who'd said something particularly dumb about *The Big Book of Useless Saturdays.*

"The receptionist is explaining that she wasn't always a receptionist in a doctor's office," my mother said, to me, her voice as dead as her eyes.

"Who's Donaldson?" I said to the receptionist, by way of apologizing for my mother's rude way of referring to her as "the receptionist," but also because I wanted to know who Donaldson was.

But the receptionist didn't respond. "I didn't ask for it," she said instead. "I was only there to interview Donaldson. For the *Tribune.* A few words, on his new play. That was all I wanted. 'Tell me, Mr. Donaldson,' I said to him, but before I could finish the question, he said, 'Lauren, it's serendipity.' I hadn't even told him my name. Still, Donaldson knew it. He said, 'Lauren, it's serendipity. Do you believe in serendipity?' And of course I said yes. Because after all he was Donaldson. 'I want you to be my amanuensis, Lauren,' Donaldson said to me. Although I'd just met him. And I was only twenty-three years old. Just a girl. And Donaldson was a lion, an aged lion. Although still handsome, yes. Although of course there was nothing between us. Although on the other hand of course there was. After all, he was Donaldson," she said, and then paused to stroke her shiny blood colored scarf, before continuing. "Donaldson said, 'I want you to be my amanuensis. And I also want you to edit my letters. I want you to collect them and I want you to edit them and after I die I want you to publish them.'" The receptionist then paused, and looked down at something in front of her. I leaned over, expecting to see Donaldson's papers, but no, only a tan folder, with my mother's name on the tab. "I didn't ask for it. I did not ask for it. That's what I said to Donaldson. I said, 'I'm here for an interview.' And Donaldson said, 'No, Lauren.' And I hadn't even told him my name. And I asked, 'Then why am I here?' Which is of course the kind of question Donaldson liked. Because it was a question only Donaldson could answer, although of course he could only answer it in his way. 'Serendipity,' Donaldson told me."

Just then the office's automatic doors slid open and through it walked a man wearing a dark blue jumpsuit and a dark blue baseball hat, and carrying a tiny vacuum cleaner. He nodded at the receptionist, Lauren, then proceeded to the fish tank, into which he inserted a long thin tube and with it began gently, hummingly, sucking along the mucky edges of the tank while the bright blue fish swam in tight circles in the center.

"Now, ma'am, what did you do for a living?" Lauren then asked my mother. This surprised me: I assumed that she'd been talking about Donaldson—who I was guessing was a famous writer that I'd never heard of—precisely because she knew my mother was a writer who'd written a famous book. But apparently, no, that too was serendipity.

"My mother is a writer," I said, and named her famous book.

"That book changed my life!" is what I wished Lauren would have said.

"Were you influenced by Donaldson?" is what she said instead.

15)

"What do you *do* all day?" my father wanted to know. This was a Saturday, a year or so after his talk in Monterey. He was calling from the Royal Tern's four star link style golf resort in Aberdeen, Scotland, just after addressing the annual gathering of the unionized hospice care workers of northern New England.

"I have a job" is what I could have said. Because this was true and my father knew it, although it wasn't really a job worth remembering, or mentioning, or describing, or doing, and the only thing that could really be said in its favor was that I could and usually did do the job while watching television.

"I watch television" is what I also could have said. "Not curing cancer" is what I said instead, because I thought I knew that that's what my father meant by his question.

"I didn't exactly cure cancer, either," my father said, and there it was: He had done something no one else had done, and he was loved for it, and it was still not enough and he hated himself for it. It was almost enough to make you swear never to do anything at all, if you were going to be this let down after you'd done it.

"Where's Mom?" I asked.

"Finishing her book," he said.

"Her book?" I said. Because this is the first I'd heard of it. Before she'd retired and followed my father around, my mother had been an accountant at a national tax filing franchise. She had never been a writer, or even a reader, as far as I knew. "What's it about?"

"How bored and unfulfilled she is, following me around while I give inspirational talks about how I didn't exactly cure cancer."

"Have you read it?"

"I have."

"How is it?"

"Better than not exactly curing cancer," my father said. "Dinner time," he added, and then hung up and went to the Royal Tern's famous salmon and lamb buffet, where he ate and ate until eventually, later, on Grand Cayman island, he died of gout, the disease of kings.

16)

Through the window I watch the reporter stick a microphone in my son's face, but then one of the girls—the one who'd helped my son to his feet and who I assume was the one who'd knocked him down in the first place—pushes my son to the ground, then kicks him in the ribs until he rolls over once, twice, and then she stands in his former spot.

I take four steps toward the window and open it. Or try to. It doesn't give and doesn't give and I wonder how long it's been since I've opened it, if I ever have, and then a whistle sounds on the television set, to my right, and then I try again and the window opens. I once, on television, watched the grounds crew roll a piece of a turf onto the football field, eight hands furiously pushing the roll until it overwhelmed the thing that had been underneath it. That's what the air feels like as it enters my living room.

"Why don't you ever ask *us* any questions?" the girl is saying to the reporter and her microphone. She points at herself and then the other girls, and says, "We are *people.* We have *names.* We have *things to say.*" Which is of course was exactly what my mother was pointing out about herself in *The Big Book of Useless Saturdays.*

17)

"There's something I don't understand." This said by a man in the audience during the question and answer period immediately following my mother's soldout reading from *The Big Book of Saturdays* at Lincoln Center in New York City. I wasn't in the audience. I was watching it at home, on Book TV. The camera was on my mother, standing behind the podium. She was squinting into the audience, her reading glasses on top of her curly head of dyed black hair. The camera never panned to the man and so it seemed as though he was speaking from some remote location—the abyss, or the afterlife. *Dad,* I thought—because in fact my father was dead by now, had two weeks before this been found in his suite at the Bayview Biltmore on Grand Cayman island, his swollen bare feet up on the coffee table, a large, tinfoil takeout roasting pan full of conch fritter poutine on his stomach. And in fact there were lots of things my father didn't understand about my mother and her book.

But this man's voice was not my father's: My father's voice was deep, avuncular, whereas this man's voice was whispy. It sounded like he was speaking through his beard hair.

"Your book is . . ." the man said, and then paused, and I pictured him flipping over the book to quote directly from the jacket copy ". . . 'an inspirational story of a woman triumphing over adversity.'" The man paused to let my mother confirm this, but my mother continued squinting at him, with her mouth screwed up, and said nothing. "But what adversity? You got to travel the world. You got to see places that most people can only dream about seeing. And you had no obligations. Your husband had to work and give his speeches and you could do whatever you wanted."

"That's right," my mother said. "And what I wanted to do was write *The Big Book of Useless Saturdays.*"

18)

My mother and I had taken our seats near the fish tank, which looked the same as it had before the cleaning, except the fish seemed stunned, dull, not swimming, just sort of floating in the tank, an inch below the surface. "If I wanted to tell the receptionist that I was a writer," my mother said, through her teeth, "I would have told her myself."

"*Was* a writer?" is what I didn't say.

"The doctor will see you now" is what Lauren the receptionist said instead.

19)

"My name is Linus," the girl who knocked my son down is telling the microphone, the camera. She points at the other girls, one by one, saying, "That's Lyle, that's Lionel, that's Lemuelson, that's Llewllyn, that's Leland, and Lester, which is spelled LEICESTER, but you'll have to trust me is pronounced Lester."

The reporter looks sideways at the cameraman, who shrugs. What to make of this, these girls, these names? Are they joking? Are they serious? Are they friends? Are they relatives? Are they sisters? Where are their parents? Where exactly in the neighborhorhood do they live?

Where do they come from? What are they *doing* here? I don't know, but then, I don't have to know. That's not my job. My job is to have the backyard where they play football with my son. I'm not the one with the camera, the microphone.

"Those are old man names," the reporter finally says, to Linus.

"Not anymore," Linus says, and the reporter laughs.

"Did I say something funny," Linus says, deadpan, and the girls laugh this time, but the reporter doesn't. She dips her head, sheepishly, as though she's been accused, maybe justly, she doesn't know, she hasn't decided yet, which is exactly how I imagine my father looking when he first read the first part of the first draft of *The Big Book of Useless Saturdays.*

Meanwhile, my son has gotten to his feet and is standing behind the girls, who are between him and the cameraman and the reporter, who are ignoring him. I can tell that my son doesn't like this one little bit. He turns and kicks the ball, in anger, toward the northwest corner of the yard, then trots after it. Picks up the ball, and when he turns around, to face them, and in the distance, me, I can see from his bright eyes that he has an idea. An idea that I doubt I'll like, any more than my father liked my mother's.

"Don't," I mouth at him, and he smiles that smile again, the one he smiles when he thinks I must be joking.

"Hey," he then yells, at the girls, and the cameraman and the reporter, "you guys want to see what's buried in this hole?"

20)

"Dad, why did Mom leave?" my son wanted to know, on the morning after his mom left.

"Because I keep digging up and burying the Walther in the backyard."

"Dad, why did you keep digging up and burying the Walther in the backyard even though Mom wanted you to stop?"

"Because I *can't* stop."

"Dad . . ." my son started to say, but I interrupted him.

"Do you know why people watch and play football?" I asked him, and he smiled that smile and said, "You must be joking," and when I said that I wasn't, he said, "You're just trying to distract me."

"Distraction," I said, turning on the television. "Yes, that's exactly why."

21)

My mother called me right after I watched her on Book TV.

"Are you still at Lincoln Center?" I asked.

"What?"

"I just finished watching you on Book TV. You were at Lincoln Center. Like, a minute ago. You must be still there."

My mother paused. I sensed that she was waiting for me to say something. "I'm going out to play football with the neighborhood girls," my son yelled from somewhere in the house, and then I heard a door slam and then a second later, watching through the window, I saw a football fly through the air, and then out of my frame of vision.

"I was at Lincoln Center three months ago," my mother said.

"But you were just there on television," I said.

"The show was taped," my mother said.

I considered this for a while. Everything I'd thought while watching Book TV now had to be updated. Or, backdated. My head hurt, and so with the hand not holding the phone to my ear I held my head, and I held it and I thought, there is nothing wrong with you, there is nothing wrong with you, which only made me even more certain that there was something wrong with me.

"So when I was watching this, Dad was still alive."

"When I was at Lincoln Center your dad was still alive."

"That's what I said," I said, although even I knew that wasn't what I'd said.

"But when you were watching it on television, your father was dead."

"But when I was watching it on television, I thought it was also happening at the same time in real life."

"In real life, your dad is also dead."

By this point, I'd switched over to the football game. Which actually was over. The on field reporter was interviewing a large man in shoulder pads. In his right hand he held his helmet. His left hand and arm were around the shoulders of a cheerleader. Apparently, he'd just proposed to her after the big win, and she'd accepted. "I've loved her ever since I was twenty years old," said the large man in pads, who looked like he was probably no older than twenty-one years old.

"Do you miss Dad?" is what I didn't to say to my mother.

"Because I miss Dad" is what I didn't say, also.

"Son," my mother said, instead. "I think there's something wrong with me. I don't feel well. I think I need you to take me to the doctor."

This surprised me. "I just saw you on Book TV. You seemed totally healthy."

22)

"There's definitely something there," the doctor said. He looked nothing like my father: young, big eyed, slender. He was wearing khaki pants, white oxford shirt, plain blue tie, running sneakers, and the kind of watch that tells you how many miles you've walked. He shirtsleeves were rolled up to the elbow, and his forearms looked like tan sticks with veins popping out. He was pointing at something on his computer screen, a picture of something inside my mother. "See it?" he said, and put his finger on the screen, obscuring what it is he wants us to see.

"I don't want to see it" is what I didn't say.

"Keep your finger right where it is" is what I didn't say, either.

"I don't need to see it" is what my mother said instead. "I know exactly what it is."

The doctor took his finger off the screen, turned on his swivel stool to more fully face my mother. "This is not a death sentence anymore," the doctor said.

"I know," my mother said. "I could live with it for a long time."

23)

From chapter twelve of *The Big Book of Useless Saturdays*:

"How long ago did Lisa K. have The Radical?" I ask my husband.

This is after his talk in the Pacific Lavender Ballroom in the Vancouver Island Kathooni Bay Resort. We are on our enclosed balcony. My husband, during his talk, spoke about Lisa K (not her real name), about her "new lease on life" (his words, not mine), about how grateful she was for him, and his world famous procedure. But now, he's talking to room service, on the phone.

"What do you mean you're out of turkey legs?" he says, tapping the menu, which of course room service can't see, although presumably they have one of their own to consult.

"Eight years," I say, answering my own question. "And how long might her new lease on life end up being?"

"Chicken wings are *not* basically the same thing as turkey legs," my husband says.

"Difficult to say," I say, again answering my own question. "And have there been side effects of The Radical procedure?"

"Two chicken wings make two chicken wings, not one turkey leg," my husband says, although I can see him doing the math, in his head, his lips moving, and I know that the ratio was close enough that he will soon be ordering two dozen chicken wings, thus coming close to the dozen turkey legs he wanted to order.

"That is not difficult to say," I say. "She has lost her hair. She has lost thirty pounds. She has lost her toenails, and her fingernails. She has lost her ability to menstruate. She has lost her sex drive. She has lost vision in her left eye. She has lost her 401(k). She has lost her house. She has lost her car. She has lost her savings, and her husband's savings, and her children's college funds."

"If what I've done is so awful," my husband says, to me, not room service, whom he has just hung up on, "why doesn't Lisa K. just stop getting the treatments?"

"I asked her the same question," I say, and I had, in the back of the Ballroom, while my husband was talking about her, Lisa K., and his famous treatment that had extended her life indefinitely. "And she said that she wanted to. That she thought about it all the time. But that whenever she mentioned it to someone, then that person said that she was a fighter, that she was an inspiration, that she shouldn't give up, that she hadn't given up yet, and that she should never give up. That as long as there was hope, as long as there was a choice, an option, then she was not allowed to give up."

"I give up," my husband says, on the phone again, talking to room service, who has called to say that they are out of chicken wings, too.

"You're not allowed give up until Lisa K. gives up," I say. But I'm not sure my husband hears me, so preoccupied is he, listening to room service telling him appromixately how many chicken fingers make a wing. "Round up," he says, to room service, and then, to me, he says, "Too late. I already have."

24)

"I already have," my mother said, after I'd told her not to give up. And then she said, "I need you to do something for me." This was after we'd been to see her doctor. We were in my living room now. My wife, who was still my wife, was out in the backyard, throwing the football around with my son, because the neighborhood girls weren't around that day. My mother was sitting on the couch next to me, holding my right hand. With my left hand I went to pick up the television remote control, which was on the couch next to me, but my mother asked me not to, said that turning on the television wasn't the thing that she needed me to do.

"But you know I don't do anything," I said. I was refusing to look at her, and instead, looked at the television screen as though there were something on it other than my shadowy, backlit reflection. "Dad became world famous for not exactly curing cancer. You became world famous for writing a book about how much you hated tagging along with him while he talked about it. You are the kind of people who do things. I'm the other kind of person."

"I was another kind of person, too," my mother said. "Until I became this kind." She reached into her handbag, which was in her lap, and withdrew a handgun. It was a dull black, all of it—handle, barrel—except for a small red dot toward the back that seemed to glow, like the red light on the television set that told you it was not yet on.

"What is that?" I said.

"It's a Walther," she said.

"Where'd you get it?"

"It was your father's," my mother said. "He was going to kill himself with it. But he decided to use the gout instead."

"No," I said. Because I now knew what she wanted me to do.

"I'd do it myself. But . . ." She didn't finish the sentence, but I knew what she was going to say anyway: that she couldn't shoot herself for the same reason my father couldn't shoot himself: because they would then become the people who become famous for giving people hope, for telling them not to quit, and who then lost hope, who then quit.

"Just let the cancer do it," I said.

"But that could take too long," my mother said.

"Just get The Radical," I said, and my mother cough-laughed, a sound much more painful than mirthful.

"But that could take forever," my mother said.

"No way," I said.

"Do you love me?" she asked.

"You're the only parent I have left" is what I wanted to say.

"Yes, so much" is what I wanted to say, also.

"I refuse to answer that question" is what I said instead.

"If you love me," my mother said, "then you'll do what I need you to do."

"No way," I said again. But it was too late: I was already thinking of a way, the way my parents had also thought of a way. "We could pretend it was a robbery, at your house," I said.

"A break-in," my mother said, nodding. She leaned back into the couch and closed her eyes, already thinking, I think, of what a relief it would be not to be sick forever.

"But what would I do with the Walther?" I asked, and just then I heard a moan coming from the dining room, which was next to the living room. I looked over and there were my wife and son. She was holding him, in her arms, like she was about to carry him over some threshold. Her eyes were big, and his were, too, and so I knew that they'd heard what my mother and I were talking about.

25)

No one is talking out in the backyard. The girls and the cameraman and the reporter just watch, silent, mesmerized, as my son attacks the hard, cold ground with his shovel.

26)

My wife turned around and carried our son through the living room and into the kitchen. I followed them. My mother stayed in the living room.

When I got to the kitchen my wife was standing there, still holding my son. The light on the stove clock blinked and blinked and the refrigerator's icemaker made its ray gun noise, followed by the sound of a single cube clunking into the bin.

"It's OK, it's just talk" is what I didn't say.

"She's just a scared old woman with cancer" is what I didn't say, also.

"Am I really going to do this?" is what I said instead.

My wife didn't say anything right away. Instead, she looked at the ceiling. I'd known her for so long, and so I knew looking at the ceiling was what she did before then saying to me, You must be joking.

"You should probably do *something*" is what she said instead, and there it was: She was saying I never did *anything*, which was not totally true—I watched television and sometimes I did my job while I also watched television—but it was true enough.

"Besides, do you love your mom?" my son said, and then he looked up at his own mother, and smiled, winningly, the way he looked and smiled into the camera while being interviewed in our backyard before, or during, or after playing football.

"Yes," I said.

"Then you you should do what she wants you to do."

"It's the right thing," my wife agreed, her voice much kinder than it had been when she'd said I should probably do *something*. "And then it'll all be over."

And when my wife said that, it felt like it was already all over, and this huge feeling of relief rushed through me, although of course nothing was over yet. I hadn't even decided what to do with the Walther afterward.

"But what do I do with the Walther afterward?" I asked.

"God, you're heavy," my wife said, to my son. She gently let him down until he was standing, his right foot on the floor, his left dangling just above it. "He sprained his ankle," she said, to me.

"Yeah," my son said, to me, his voice heavy with meaning. "I stepped in a hole, in the backyard."

27)

My husband puts down the manuscript, takes off his glasses, rubs his eyes with his fists, takes his fists away. His eyes look like little blue pencil erasers in between the pillows of his cheeks. He's lying on the bed, feet like almost-burst sausages peeking out from underneath the sheets. I'm sitting on a chair, next to the sliding glass door, that leads out to the lanai that leads out to the cedar plank path that leads out to the private beach next to the private eighteen hole course at the Key Biscayne Coconut Grove Majestic. I am waiting for my husband to say that this, the final draft of my book, is bad, although I know it's good.

"Why do we hurt the people we love?" my husband says instead, and I don't answer, because he knows why.

"So I make you feel like you don't exist," my husband says, and picks up my book and waves it at me.

"Whether you make me feel that way or not, that's the way I feel."

My husband nods. He may not have totally cured cancer, and I may not love him, or at least love him enough not to publish my book, but he's a good man, and he and I both know this book will begin to kill him before the gout finishes the job. But still he says, "So publish your book and make yourself feel that you exist."

And I did. And now I do.

Thus ending *The Big Book of Useless Saturdays.*

28)

"Please just do it," my mother said, her voice booming, out of the darkness, because I'd told her I couldn't do this with the lights on, couldn't do this if I had to look at her face, although her voice reminded me of her book which reminded me of her face, which meant it was like I *was* looking at her, the person that I loved, my mother, my last parent, and then I couldn't do it, not even with the lights off.

I turned the lights on. There my mother was, eyes closed, sitting in her chair, clutching the arms of the chair like she was preparing for liftoff.

"I won't" is what I didn't say.

"I can't" is what I didn't say, either.

"Just give me the gun" is what my mother said instead. She extended her right hand and into it I placed the Walther, and she curled her fingers around the butt like a seasoned gunslinger. My mother still hadn't opened her eyes. For a while neither of us said or did anything, for so long that I thought, with relief, that my mother wouldn't be able to do it either, which meant that we were even, equal, the same, and that now that neither of us could do what she'd wanted me to do, we could live out the rest of our long lives together, even though my life would almost certainly be longer, and better, and then she opened her eyes and said . . . nothing, just looked at me one last time and then shot herself in the head. I won't describe it, except to say that when my head stopped pounding with the noise of the shot and my nose stopped itching with the smell of the cordite and my eyes stopped crying at the sight of what was left of my mother, I felt so alone—it was just me and the gun now. I picked it up off the floor where she'd dropped it, ran out of that house, to my own, where my wife and son were waiting for me.

"Did you really do it?" my wife said, and I could hear the skepticism in her voice, and that felt bad.

"Mom, of course he did it. Look, he's carrying the gun," my son said, and I could hear the pride in his voice, and that felt better.

"Let's just do this" is what I wanted to say, and then that's what I did say. The three of us went into the backyard. My wife had the shovel. She handed it to me and I dug and dug while she and my son watched, and when the hole was deep enough I dropped the Walther into it, and then with the shovel I filled in the hole, and then we went to bed. The next day, after we heard the news, after we talked to the police, after they told me that they hadn't found the gun, but they were sure it was a robbery, a break-in gone wrong, after they'd said they were sorry, that they'd be in touch, I thought, to myself, well, that's it, it's all over. I walked out into the yard. It was a big yard, with lots of trees, and lots of rocks and piles of brush and leaves, surrounding lots of lawn. I looked at the spot where we'd buried the gun. After I'd filled in the hole we'd covered it with compost. The night before it seemed like we'd hid the hole as well as anyone could have. But in the daylight, no: The compost looked suspicious, like a beard that seemed like it might not be real. It wasn't exactly right. I could do better, I thought. There were better places in the yard to dig the hole, better ways to hide it.

"What're you looking at?" said a voice behind me. I turned. It was the girl I now know to be Linus, surrounded by the rest of the girls. Through the window I'd watched them play football with my son, in my backyard, a dozen times, but this was the first time, the only time, I'd stood in my backyard with them. The air was electric, the way it gets right before there's some violent change in wind, or weather. The way I'd imagined being on a real football field would feel. I did my best to look at Linus, and not at where I'd buried the Walther.

"He's looking at the neighborhood's best backyard football field," my son said, running into the yard, a football in his right hand.

"Bull," Linus said. "He was looking at that pile of stuff over there."

My son looked at me, and I looked at him.

"I'm never going to be able to stop burying and reburying the Walther" is what I didn't say.

"Please help me" is what I didn't say either.

"What pile of stuff?" my son said instead, to Linus. And by saying that, he was saying, to me, "Don't worry, Dad. We're in this together. I love you." He tossed the ball to Linus, toward her face, and she was not entirely looking at him, but still, she caught it, and grinned, and said, pointing the football at my son, "I'm going to knock the *shit* out of you," and suddenly, you could tell, everyone had forgotten all about what it was I'd been really looking at.

29)

"Am I looking at what I think I'm looking at?" Linus asks, while the camerman and the reporter try to push her and the other girls out of the way, to get a better shot of the Walther in the hole.

"Yup," my son says.

"Whose is it?"

My son turns to look at me, with a blank determined look on his face, and I know he's going to tell them, and I know why. Because this was the answer to my father's question: We hurt the people we love because they kind of ask us to.

And then my son turns away from me and I close the window and see what's on television. Another football game is starting. It's a Saturday. You could watch games all day and night, if you needed to.

CHEST BUMP

Jane's husband wanted to own and operate a drive-thru broth restaurant. His name was Barry. He was a man of enthusiasms. He had once driven thousands of miles to buy the most expensive Rottweiler puppy in the whole United States of America and had named it Chest Bump. He and Jane had gotten into a fight over the whole thing—the expense, and the drive, although not the name. Jane was, in fact, not crazy about the dog's name. But she was too tired after fighting over the money and the miles to also then fight about the stupid name. *Chest Bump.* Not that she was without her own enthusiasms. Six years earlier, right after the arrival of Chest Bump, she had stopped taking her birth control pills without telling Barry and nine months later she gave birth to their daughter.

The dog was gone now—it had been poisoned. But they still had the daughter. *Ilsa.*

"No," Jane said to Barry, about the broth restaurant, knowing it was too late, that he'd already done it.

"Too late," Barry said. "I've already done it."

Why didn't she just leave him! Well, first he used to be handsome, and then later they'd had this baby together, and now there was this broth place, which evidently—for reasons Barry couldn't quite explain, the reasons were complicated, they had to do with the legal system, of course, and also money, which, between the two of them, Jane had significantly more of—was actually in her name. How Barry had done this without her signature was a mystery. They had separate checking accounts. To prevent this kind of thing from happening, again. Jane really was going to leave him, someday soon, maybe it would be this day, maybe today was the day. Today! She would leave him today! But first, Barry was insisting he drive her to check out their new broth restaurant.

They lived in a beautiful part of the world. But they rarely saw the beauty, which was the Atlantic Ocean. They were more likely to smell it than see it. Jane rolled down the front passenger window of the Subaru. There *was* a smell out there. Jane supposed it was the ocean. But right then, it smelled like broth. She did not mention this to Barry. He would point out that when he'd managed the gun range the ocean had smelled like cordite, and when he'd worked as a hospital orderly the ocean had smelled like bandaids.

Jane was already an owner and operator of a business. Since well before they'd gotten married, she'd made and sold chocolate in the shape of animals. Bear. Deer. Moose. Lobsters. Clams. Only creatures native to their beautiful cold part of the world. She was working on the American bald eagle right now. The head was white chocolate and the torso and wings were dark chocolate. She had made the tail feathers out of white chocolate, too, and she knew she was right to do so, because the tail feathers on the real eagle were white, but still it worried her. Everyone knew about the white head. But she was afraid no one would know about the real tail feathers, and they would either accuse her of getting it wrong, or of showing off by insisting on getting right this obscure detail of the famous bird.

"You remember the cow," Barry was saying. It was as though he were reading her thoughts! Except that she had never made a cow out of chocolate. Jane had decided early on that she would not include animals raised for slaughter in her line of chocolates, and despite a surprisingly high number of customers wondering where were the pigs, she had stuck with that decision.

In fact, Barry was not even talking to Jane. He was talking to Ilsa, on the car's speakerphone. Ilsa was in kindergarten, half day. It was November. She had been in school for two months now. And still, not a half day went by when Ilsa didn't call home from somewhere in the school—the nurse's office, the principal's office, it seemed to be a different office and a different phone each time—with some well-considered argument about why school was not the proper learning environment for her and would they come and pick her up, forever.

Whatever Barry had been saying about the cow, now he was listening to Ilsa. Her voice, coming out of the car's dashboard, was squeaky and high-pitched but also reasonable, like a doll that was also a lawyer and arguing a case in a courtroom, a tiny courtroom inside their car's dashboard. "What I miss in my classroom is a sense of play and discovery," she said. Barry listened; he nodded; he nodded some more. Jane often had to talk him out of doing what Ilsa wanted them to do. Often what Ilsa wanted him to do was the exact opposite of what Jane wanted him to do. She now wondered if in fact this broth restaurant had been Ilsa's idea, and not Barry's.

Did Jane love Barry? She guessed she did. But why? Well, she loved that he loved their daughter so much. Actually, this was the kind of thing her friends said about their husbands. As though this—the loving of one's own child so much—were some incredible accomplishment that needed to be paid special attention to. Although you couldn't say something like that without you yourself being suspected of not loving your child so much. So, OK, Jane loved that Barry loved their daughter so much. But what were the other reasons? Oh, she was sure that she had them. She just had to try hard to think of them, sometimes.

And did Jane love Ilsa? Well, that had been the idea. But Ilsa had made that difficult. She was a lawyerly child, but before that she had been a very angry baby. In fact, that had been Jane's nickname for Ilsa: "The Very Angry Baby." Sometimes, she called her "Devil Baby." Sometimes, she combined the two nicknames and called her "The Very Angry Devil Baby." Mostly for the way she screamed—screamed when she wanted to go to bed, screamed when she didn't want to go to bed, screamed when she was in the car, or being put in the car, or being taken out of the car. Her scream was distinctly nonhuman, nonanimal—metallic, if it was anything.

Jane had a friend, Charlotte. Charlotte had led an interesting life full of criminal acts that had gone spectacularly wrong but that she still somehow had not been caught at or arrested for. Once when Charlotte was over to the house and Ilsa did not want to take a nap that she was supposed to take and was screaming like a Very Angry Devil Baby about it, Charlotte told Jane about the time that Charlotte had stolen a safe from the convenience store and then, in an attempt to open it, ran over the safe with her car right there in the convenience store parking lot, except that not only did that not open the safe, but the safe then got stuck under the car, and Charlotte was then forced to flee the scene, the safe making sparks on the pavement and ruining the car's undercarriage. Ilsa's screaming was like the sound of a safe being dragged at thirty-five miles per along frozen blacktop underneath a 1988 Chevy Lumina, Charlotte said.

Ilsa suddenly hung up. This happened sometimes. The call would end with no warning and no explanation. Just with a click and the violent buzzing of the dial tone. It didn't worry Jane. Usually, Ilsa would call back later, presumably from a different phone in a different room, and restart the conversation right where it had ended.

Jane wanted to know more about this cow business, but not enough to ask. She knew that if she asked, she would get an explanation and then it would upset her and then Barry would say, "Well, you asked."

"I really think you ought to reconsider this broth thing, Barry," Jane said. She scooched down in her seat and stuck her feet out the window. She liked this for the reckless feeling it gave her, although as far as she knew the maneuver had never resulted in anyone getting a foot or toe severed, or even scratched. It probably wasn't even illegal.

"When people think of broth," Barry said, "they usually think chicken." This was so. Jane herself had been thinking chicken. "But I think people will be surprised by our amazing variety of broths."

Again, Jane had to stop herself from asking about the amazing variety. Instead, she asked how the broth was to be served.

"There'll be cups," Barry said. His long hair used to sweep back and up in an especially dramatic way, but lately Jane had noticed that it sort of stopped before it got started and hung there, above his forehead, like a question mark reflected in a mirror. "But the cups will look like little thermoses."

Jane tried and failed to picture this. "Do you mean they'll actually *be* little thermoses?"

Barry nodded, as though this was the idea all along, although Jane wondered if he'd thought of it only just now after she'd mentioned the possibility. "But not *too* little," he said.

There was the time Barry was this close to inventing a microwave that could sterilize eggs. And then he wanted to bring bingo into the twenty-first century. A design and business plan for mass marketing a potentially less off-putting crucifix. A special mirror for men who liked to cut their own hair. A karate studio featuring a more authentic kind of karate that ended up being virtually indistinguishable from the kind of karate everyone already thought they knew all about. A home ropemaking studio. Those three player pianos. The player pianos had been advertised in the local pennysaver: They were to be purchased all together, or not at all. Barry had had no specific plan for them, but he'd had a vision of all of them arranged in a triangle, all those keys, rising and falling on their own, as though in conversation with each other, it was captivating. Barry couldn't get the image out of his head. But neither, once he'd purchased them, could he get the pianos to work, not even one of them, and it wasn't meant to be.

And what about Chest Bump? Actually, Chest Bump had turned out OK. Affectionate to everyone. Good tempered. More or less did what you told him to do, and was satisfyingly cowed whenever he did something that caused his owners' disapproval. Which wasn't often. Barry had driven too far to get him and had spent too much money on him and had given him that dumb name. But that was not the dog's fault. No, Chest Bump had been a pretty good dog.

And had Jane loved Chest Bump? Not exactly, but she definitely hadn't hated him, either.

Ilsa was back on the phone now.

"Wait, what cow?" Ilsa wanted to know. This, Jane thought, was why she'd wanted a child so badly: so that the child could ask the questions that Jane herself did not feel like asking but still wanted to know the answers to. And look, the child had done what she'd wanted the child to do! But that had turned out not to be enough.

"On the roof," Barry said.

Jane knew now where they were headed. There had been a drive-thru coffee shop in town, just on the edge of town, on the four-lane commercial strip leading to the interstate. It had been stuck between two car dealerships. Actually, they were owned by the same car-dealing family, but one sold one brand of car and the other sold another. When Jane had been a child, these two different brands of cars had been rivals. Boys in her classes had argued violently about the superiority of one or the other, even though none of the boys, at this stage in their lives, was old enough to drive.

Anyway, the drive-thru coffee shop, which had some time ago gone out of business, was small, just large enough for one person and the cups and coffeemakers and whatnot, and was painted purple, and on its roof was a white and black cow, sitting, with its legs crossed, wearing polka-dotted bloomer and a floppy hat on its head and a daisy sticking out of the hat. Jane had never determined the thinking behind the cow. The coffee shop's name included no bovine puns. Possibly the cow had been a leftover from the last failed business that had occupied that odd, tiny building.

Jane knew, and knew Barry knew, that Ilsa loved that cow. Sometimes she would make them drive out of their way just to get yet another look at its bloomers.

A squeal came out of the car's speakers and into the car. The squeal was Ilsa's, and it was happy, but it still reminded Jane, as many things did, of those terrible noises that Ilsa had made when she was a Very Angry Devil Baby.

"I wish you wouldn't call her that," Barry had said. This was four years earlier, on their front steps, during the era when Barry had started his own pest control business, which was different from the well-known national firms in that he forsook the usual chemicals and instead used more benign household items to kill rats and mice and so on. That day the distant ocean breeze had smelled of plaster of paris and instant potatoes.

Jane had just told Barry about Charlotte's story of the safe and Ilsa's screaming. Ilsa wasn't screaming at that moment, and instead was sitting placidly on her father's lap, and in fact almost never screamed when Barry was around, which was maybe why he didn't appreciate, let alone understand, the nickname.

"The Very Angry Devil Baby?" Jane had said. She'd paused, as though to make sure they were talking about same nickname. "It's a funny nickname."

But in truth she hadn't been entirely sure about that. At that time, she hadn't been entirely sure about anything. It was Ilsa's screaming: It had made everything indistinct, fuzzy. Things Jane had never doubted before she had now begun to doubt.

Jane's own chocolates, for instance. She'd thought the animals were the same as ever, but customers had been complaining, about the clams in particular, which, the customers said, looked more ragged than scalloped.

And then there had been Barry himself. He was proud of his exterminator's outfit, which was basically a dark green jumpsuit, with his name in white cursive over his right pectoral. He'd liked to wear the jumpsuit even when he wasn't working. He'd been wearing it at that moment, sitting on their front steps, with his daughter on his lap, Chest Bump at his feet. Jane had thought he'd looked ridiculous. Especially since he barely had any real customers. People wanted their pests to be cured by real poison. The kind of poison that would kill the people themselves. That's how you knew it was real. But other people seemed quite attracted to the jumpsuit. Barry's former girlfriends, for instance. They'd ignored him for years, but now, they kept driving by the house, wondering how things were, what he'd been up to, how much time had it been since they'd run into each other, things of that vague and suspicious nature.

"It's just a funny little nickname," Jane had insisted anyway.

"I just wish you wouldn't call her that," Barry had repeated, and at that moment the most recent of his former girlfriends drove past, slowed, waved hello, said something that Jane couldn't quite catch, but seemed to be some kind of brief praise song for Barry's jumpsuit, then waved goodbye and drove off. Jane was not a jealous person. Not about Barry. Whom she always assumed she would leave one day; it had never occurred to her that the opposite might happen instead. But Jane had watched Barry wave goodbye to his former girlfriend, and to Jane's surprise she thought that Barry really did look sort of attractive, with his rich green jumpsuit and his smiling baby girl on his lap, and his big broad-chested, blockheaded dog named Chest Bump at his feet.

Ilsa's delighted squeal had evidently given her away. Jane heard what sounded like a voice of authority in the background, some teacher or principal, and once again their connection was severed.

Meanwhile, Jane could see the cow. It grew closer and closer, you could not not see it, it was like a water tower, or a lighthouse, and suddenly they were in the shadow of the thing. The pavement on which you were to drive-thru was cracked and weed ridden, and the cow and building itself looked faded and rained on. There was a big for sale or lease sign out front. There was nothing to indicate that the building had been sold, was under contract, anything like that. This gave Jane hope. The sign, like the building, looked weary.

Jane and Barry got out of the car and stood there, regarding the building, but before either of them could say anything about it, a man walked over to them from the car dealership to the right of the cow. He appeared to be wearing a black suit, but when he got closer Jane noticed that the pants were a slightly lighter black color than the jacket, and that the two pieces of clothing were made of different fabric, too. Jane wondered who, exactly, this guy thought he was fooling.

"Tom Morgan," the man said, shaking their hands. Morgan was the name attached to the car dealerships. Tom Morgan wore a thick, bristly salt and pepper mustache. There was the faint smell of tuna salad about him. "I sincerely hope you good folks aren't considering buying or leasing this place of business. This sad, cursed place. It's like the country of Armenia, or also certain professional sports teams. Car manufacturers whose passenger pickups suffer from congenitally tricky low idles. I don't want to slander our competitors. But, your Dodges, and your Mazdas. Men whose first names are shorthand for the male reproductive organ. Rod. Dick. I don't need to go on. Just really really cursed. We Morgans have been selling cars and trucks on these non-adjacent lots for fifty-three years. How often has this building between our two dealerships come up for sale? I don't think we've kept official records, but let me assure you it's been many times. Have I been tempted? Well, sure. My brother is in charge of Lot B, and you can ask him if he's been similarly tempted and he'll tell you that of course he has. He doesn't like it when we call his lot 'Lot B,' but it is a more recent lot. But the short answer is, it's been tempting. Buy the building. Knock it down. Pave it over. Put up a new building. Or tear up the pavement, just install some attractive green space. Bring the two parts of our family dealership together that have until now been cleaved, or at least kept asunder. But no, I won't do it. I've seen too many businesses fail here, too many lives ruined. Would you buy a haunted house? A home where a mother has in desperation drowned her young children in the bathtub and then hanged herself in that same bathroom using the shower rod and an extension cord? I see you grimace at that, miss. As you should. I want you to know that if you buy this place then you will end up picturing an extension cord around you and your husband's necks for the rest of your miserable days. Please just walk away."

"We've already bought it," Barry said.

"Then you'll find that we're good neighbors," Tom Morgan said, crossed from their property to his, where he then strolled through the rows of cars, occasionally bending at the waist and pretending to find and then remove some speck of dust on a gleaming bumper.

The kitchen, in the dark, had seemed otherworldly. Jane hadn't been sure how she'd gotten there. Slowly, she'd taken inventory of the familiar objects that seemed so alien: There were the glowing digits on the microwave; there was the soft snoring of Chest Bump there on his big bed in the corner; there was the spaceship hum of the refrigerator, the ray gun noise of ice cubes being made before they clunked into the bin; there was Barry's jumpsuit, hanging on the back of the closet door, looking in that dark room like something you'd put on before rocketing into space. Underneath the jumpsuit, on the floor, was Barry's plastic sprayer bottle of homemade all-natural pest control. She'd often asked Barry to safely store it, but this he could never seem to remember to do.

Isla had just then screamed, from nearby. Not merely from nearby. From Jane's arms. And then Jane had come to herself. She was of course in the kitchen. Holding Ilsa. Who'd probably been screaming in her bed. Jane had no doubt taken her out, had walked with her down into the kitchen, that comforting domestic space. But no, it had not worked, Ilsa was still screaming, screaming like . . . well, never mind. In truth, Jane herself had by now gotten tired of the nickname. It had ceased to make her feel better. Ilsa's screaming had created the nickname, had created the need for the nickname, and now had ruined the nickname. Obliterated it. Much like she had obliterated the soothing kitchen noises with her screaming. Even the dog, who was a deep sleeper, had stopped snoring and was looking in their direction with his head up.

And Barry? Afterward, Jane had no memory of where Barry had been. She supposed he'd been asleep. Barry was an even deeper sleeper than Chest Bump. Barry could sleep through anything. One of those things people inexplicably insisted on bragging about, like loving your children so much.

After their conversation with Tom Morgan, Barry's face looked like it had when he'd found Chest Bump on the floor that next morning, dead, with bloody foam about its mouth and nostrils, right next to the tipped over and spilled out sprayer bottle of homemade poison. Jane had seen then, and could see now, these things flitter across Barry's face: Bewilderment. Accusation. Blame. Guilt. Regret. Despair. Terror. Shame. Failure. Loss. Inevitability. Acceptance. Eternity.

"I'm not going to leave you today" is what Jane wanted to say.

"Is it too late to get out of it?" is what she said instead.

"Probably not," Barry admitted. This had ended up being true of so many of his enthusiasms. The paperwork hadn't yet gone through. The bank had had smart second thoughts. There was already a less gruesome crucifix on the market and doing well. Even the player pianos.

Barry could not fix them and his vision had remained unrealized, but he ended up advertising them in that very same pennysaver, had made back almost half of what he'd spent in the first place.

Meanwhile, Jane suddenly had a new idea about the American bald eagle's tail feathers, how the chocolates could satisfy her customers while still staying true to her realistic likeness of the bird.

The phone rang from the dashboard again, and this time it was Jane who pushed the button and picked up the call, although once again it was Ilsa who spoke first.

"My half day is over," she said, and in the background Jane could hear the happy rush and babble of children being released. "Why haven't you picked me up yet?"

It had been Jane's friend Charlotte who'd given her the idea.

"You could always poison her," Charlotte had said. This was on the telephone, in that dark kitchen. Jane had sat Ilsa on the floor, had let her scream from there, right in Chest Bump's face. Jane had made the mistake of telling Charlotte that the Very Angry Devil Baby was crying again, still, again, and she didn't know what to do about it.

"Charlotte," Jane had said. Whispered this, actually, even though it hadn't been Jane who'd mentioned the poisoning, hadn't been her idea, would never have even entered her head, probably, had Charlotte not put it there.

"I poisoned my father once," Charlotte said, not whispering at all. Jane pictured Charlotte's own kitchen, which was where she, like most people, liked to talk on the phone. The bright yellow linoleum, the garbage spilling over. She'd never looked under Charlotte's sink, but could easily see the rat poison, the Drano. Meanwhile, there, underneath Barry's jumpsuit, was that plastic sprayer bottle of homemade all-natural pest control.

"What happened?"

"I ended up poisoning my stepmom instead," Charlotte said ruefully.

"Did she die?"

"Eventually," Charlotte said. "But not from the poison."

Ilsa had started screaming even more loudly then, too loudly for Jane to carry on her conversation. She'd hung up, and turned toward her daughter, the dog, the sprayer bottle. Ilsa's face had been very close to Chest Bump's; his ears had been twitching with her noise.

Jane had picked up the sprayer bottle, bent over, pumped the pump a few times, picked up the nozzle, pointed it at her daughter's face, got right in there, as close to Ilsa's face as Ilsa's face was to Chest Bump's, and then laughed. For of course she would not do it. She would not poison her baby, and she would not leave her husband, and she made her chocolates but otherwise would not do much of anything. Jane had returned the sprayer bottle to its place, underneath Barry's jumpsuit. Ilsa was still screaming, of course. There were chunks of chocolate on the kitchen counter. Sometimes, Jane experimented with the chocolate at home before bringing it into the store. The counter was covered with half-eaten puffins, shards of harbor seals. Jane had grabbed for the chocolate in the dark, and then put a piece in Ilsa's screaming mouth, just sort of shoved it in there, with no hope if it actually working.

It had worked. Ilsa stopped screaming. She took the piece of chocolate out of her mouth, examined it. Enclosed her fist around it. Put the fist in Chest Bump's face, the way the Jane had just put the nozzle in Ilsa's, then opened her hand. Chest Bump ate what was in the hand. Chocolate was terrible for dogs. It was poison, really. Every chocolatier knew this. But of course Ilsa hadn't. Ilsa had been delighted! She'd been fascinated! She'd wanted more chocolate! Of course, Jane wasn't going to give her more. But then Ilsa opened her mouth, and Jane could already hear the sounds coming out of it, and so then of course Jane gave her more of the chocolate. She gave her all of it. And when it was done, Ilsa seemed satisfied. Jane had brought her back to bed, although on her way through the kitchen, Jane had tipped the sprayer bottle of poison onto the floor, to make it seem, to Barry, that it, and he, was to blame.

Isla climbed into the backseat of the Subaru, onto the little throne of her booster. Other children had trouble with the seatbelt, and in fact many adults had trouble with the seatbelt, and in fact Jane herself sometimes had trouble with the seatbelt, but not Ilsa. She was a competent little thing. She belted herself in, then rubbed her hands together.

"Tell me some more about our new broth restaurant," Ilsa said.

THE SLIM JIM

My husband and I took our son out to dinner for his fourteenth birthday. We'd taken him to dinner at the same restaurant for his fifth birthday, a five-year-old who had five-year-old tastes going to a very fancy adult restaurant for his fifth birthday and it could have turned out badly but it didn't and he had loved it, and we had loved him, and he had loved us, but lots of things can change in nine years, and lots of things had, including, least importantly, my husband's eyesight. He was wearing glasses now. He put them on to read the menu, took them off, held them away from his face, put them on again, brought the menu closer to his face, held it away from him. Our son, Craig, was also reading the menu, squinting angrily at the thing like *he* needed glasses, too, although he didn't. He always squinted angrily, at everything and everyone, except when it was pointed out that he was squinting angrily, and then he would bug his eyes, also angrily.

"Why is everything in *French*?" our son wanted to know. Because it's a French restaurant, I could have said, but didn't, knowing that my husband would, and soon he did. Instead I said, "So beautiful." I wasn't talking about any of us; I was talking about the restaurant, which, before it became Le Miracle, had been a Catholic church. The ceiling soared. The stained glass glowed. The grand pipes of the organ . . . didn't do anything. I was afraid for my son to notice it. Because he would then ask, "Does that thing even *work*?"

"Why is everything on this menu written in *French*?" Craig wanted to know.

"What a good question," my husband said. His deadpan was so dead that it really did sound like a corpse might have spoken. I tried not to look at him. I wanted this to be a nice night. I needed it to be a nice night. We all did, I think. It had been a long time since the three of us had had one. It had been a long time since even two out of the three of us—any two out of the three—had had one. How bad had it gotten? I sometimes flipped through photo albums, looking at the pictures of us, say, say four years earlier, fondly remembering that as the time when we actually used to say goodbye to each other before leaving the house.

Craig closed the menu, loudly, like a door. There was a mountain range of pimples on the left side of his nose, and one enormous zit that might have also been a cold sore on the right corner of his mouth. He rubbed his nose, opened and closed that side of his mouth, open and closed it, doing his very best to crack the scab.

This was one of the many things my husband nagged Craig about: his face, how he wouldn't leave it alone. I could see that my husband was fighting the urge to say something now, too. To his credit, I guess, he didn't end up saying anything, but Martin—that's my husband's name—did take off his glasses, possibly so he couldn't see our son's face anymore.

In addition to his failing eyesight, Martin was going bald. He'd already gone gray. He sometimes wore cardigans. He was wearing one now, a gray one, under his blue sport coat.

For years I'd been exercising constantly, fanatically, trying to keep somewhat in shape, and it was only just barely working, and I had started looking forward to the day when I would decide to give up and get fat, and in fact, when I'd admitted that to Martin, just a day or two before Craig's birthday dinner, in the hopes that he'd say something like, Go ahead and get fat, I'll love you anyway, Martin instead looked at me shrewdly, over his glasses, and said, "Hey, good plan."

We saw the worst in one another other, in other words, and when we weren't seeing the worst in one another other, we did everything we could to bring out, and then see, the worst in one another. I was so tired of it, and Martin and Craig must have been so tired of it, too.

"What're you going to have?" I asked Craig.

"I don't know," Craig said, and it sounded like he was going to cry and he must have heard it, too, because he picked up the menu, raised it to chin level, then dropped it on the table, bang, loudly enough so that I'm sure some of the other diners heard. The waiter had already brought over red wine for Martin and me, a Coke for Craig, and I could see him heading toward our table again, probably ready to take our order, but after Craig had dropped the menu, I saw the waiter raise an eyebrow, turn, and retreat to the kitchen. The restaurant had been loud a second earlier, but now, after Craig had dropped the menu, a funereal hush had fallen over the place.

When we'd asked Craig a week before this where he wanted to go for his birthday dinner, he'd said "Nowhere."

"We're not going *nowhere* for your birthday," Martin had said, and I'd agreed.

"That would be depressing," I'd said then.

"Why does everything have to be written in *French*?" Craig said now.

"Because this is a *French* restaurant," Martin said. He said this in French. My husband was a French major in college, and so was I: We had first met, and fell in love, during our semesters abroad in Toulouse. We had been fluent then, and we were pretty close to being fluent now, too. I'd understood what my husband said, but of course Craig hadn't: He was studying Spanish in school. "Because this is a *French restaurant*," Martin said again, in French, and I saw Craig's face turn even more murderous and I thought of how years later when people would ask their questions—why did your son kill your husband? Why did Craig kill his father?—I would think of this moment as one of the main reasons.

But no one ended up killing anyone. Instead, my husband sighed. He closed his eyes, leaned back in his chair, and told this story:

"Two years ago I decided I was going to move out of the house and into an apartment. It was an apartment right off the interstate, in one of those buildings with a billboard on top that announced that if you lived there you'd be home by now. It was just after five o'clock. I had been at work. I was coming home. And I realized, when I saw that sign, that I didn't want to come home. That I would rather go anywhere than go home, or at least the home I already had.

"So I got off the interstate, drove on the frontage road to the apartment building. It was a brand-new building. There were no lights on in it except for the lights in the rental office. There was a young guy in the office, a young, fattish guy with a goatee. He was wearing a suit, a shiny gray suit with the double-breasted jacket fully buttoned even though the jacket was way too tight and the guy was sitting down, behind his desk. I asked the guy—he was the manager—if there were any apartments available, and he laughed. 'They're all available,' he said.

"I took the first one he showed me, on the third floor, the top floor. 'The penthouse suite!' the manager said, and laughed again, and then he took my check, covering my deposit and first and last month's rent, and then he told me that water and utilities were included, and then he left. I listened to him walk down the stairs. The apartment walls and door were so thin that I could hear, three floors down, the office door open, close, then open, then close again. Then, the sound of the guy's car starting and pulling away. I never saw, or heard, him again.

"After the manager drove away I walked around my apartment. It wasn't a long walk. It was a one-bedroom apartment, with a bathroom, a living room, a kitchen that was basically just a corner of the living room, with a mini-refrigerator, a counter, a stovetop (no oven), a sink. On the nights when Craig stayed with me, I thought, I'd sleep on the pullout couch (which I'd have to buy) in the living room and he could sleep in my room. But being honest, I knew Craig would never sleep there. The whole place smelled like chemicals, like dry cleaning. I'm sure the walls, the ceilings, had just been painted, but already they were starting to crack and peel. There were soft spots everywhere in the Pergo floors, in the linoleum. I could see Craig's face when, in the near future, I showed him around the apartment. 'This is where you'll sleep,' I'd say, and then point to my bed (which I'd have to buy) and I was sure he'd say, 'Dad, no offense, but I'm never going to sleep here.'

"And I knew that. That's why I'd chosen the place: because I knew no one would ever want to be with me there, and so there would be no one to fight with, there would be no one to criticize, to nag, there would be no one to hate me, no one for me to hate, except for myself.

"I imagined myself coming to the apartment at night, after work, sitting at the table (which I'd have to buy), eating dinner and having a drink (I'd have to buy the plates and utensils and glasses, too), in complete silence. I wanted that so badly. I was so hungry for that.

"I was so hungry, period: It was dinnertime by now. There was a convenience store, a Red-E Mart, across the frontage road from my building. I walked there, bought a microwavable chicken burrito from the clerk, brought it back to my apartment. My apartment! I'd never had my own apartment before. I'd lived with my parents, and then with my roommate in college, and then with you right after college, and then us with Craig after that. But this was my own apartment! My first meal in my own apartment!

"Except my own apartment didn't have a microwave. I remembered that only when I got back there and took the burrito out of its plastic wrapper and slipped it in into its cardboard sleeve and then realized I had nothing—no microwave, no stove—to put the burrito into. No frying pan to cook it using one of the two burners. No plate to put it on, either. No utensils to cut it up with and eat that way. No, if I wanted to eat the burrito, I'd have to eat it cold, with my hands.

"So I did that. I did it to prove that I could. Because I had thought so many times of doing what I'd just done, of leaving both of you, just leaving and starting over again, but always something stopped me, always I let something—guilt, money, love—get in my way. The cold burrito was another one of those things. And I knew if I let it get in the way, if I decided that the prospect of eating an unmicrowaved microwavable burrito was too gruesome, too depressing, and that I should go home and then try again some other time, when I was better prepared, then I'd never move out, then I'd go back home and we'd all keep on making each other miserable, forever. Because we were making each other miserable. We're still making each other miserable. I wanted that to stop. I still want it to stop.

"So I ate the burrito. I removed the cardboard sleeve and ate the burrito. It was disgusting. It tasted more like a cardboard sleeve than food. I ate it anyway. To prove that I could. Which is not to say that I *enjoyed* it, that I *lingered* over it, that I *savored* it. No, by the end of the burrito, I couldn't even stand to chew the thing, and instead just swallowed it, or at least I tried to swallow it, but I didn't, or couldn't, the piece was too big to swallow and instead it got stuck in my throat.

"It got stuck there, halfway down my throat. But I wasn't choking to death on it, not exactly. I mean, I could feel the chunk of burrito in there, it was definitely there, lodged halfway down in my throat, and while I couldn't speak (I tried to yell 'Help!' but I couldn't get the word out, couldn't even make a sound loud enough to be heard by someone else in the building, not that there was anyone else in the building to hear or help me anyway) I could breathe. I stood there, in the middle of the kitchen, or kitchenette, or the part of the living room where the kitchen stuff was, breathing and breathing, just to reassure myself that I could. I could. That's why I didn't panic, at first: because at least I could breathe. Although my breathing did make a strange whistling sound, a sort of musical whistling sound as it went past, or maybe even through, the burrito.

"OK, so I wasn't choking yet. But still, I didn't feel like I could just stand there forever, not choking, breathing, but not breathing fully, not breathing right. Of course, I could have driven to the hospital. But that seemed a little dramatic, and also like a surrender, like not eating the burrito because I didn't have a microwave would have also been a surrender. No, I'd eaten the burrito, or tried to, and now I was going to have to get the burrito out of my throat, with no help, by myself, on my own.

"So I pounded my chest. I don't know why I pounded my chest—that's not where the burrito was stuck—but I did: I pounded and pounded. I don't know how long I pounded, but it was long enough for my arms to get tired, long enough for my chest to hurt the next day. Finally, I stopped. I was feeling exhausted, from all the pounding, but also, it occurred to me, because maybe I wasn't getting enough oxygen, maybe enough oxygen wasn't getting to my brain because of the burrito. The overhead fluorescent lights were buzzing and flickering. Maybe they'd always been buzzing and flickering but I only noticed them then, and the buzzing and flickering and maybe also the lack of oxygen were making my head hurt, so I turned the lights off. Then, except for the light from the tall light towers around the apartment building's parking lot coming in through my one window (I had one window), the place was completely dark. That felt better. More peaceful. Which made me wonder whether the pounding had been a mistake, and whether I should try something less violent.

"So I began massaging my throat. Just sort of gently rubbing it, like you would a child's back when he's upset, the way I used to do to Craig until that time, I forget how old he was, I forget whether he was sick or upset or both, all I remembered was that I started to rub his back and he said, 'What do you think you're *doing*?' and then he reached back and tried to slap my hand. At least I assumed that's what he tried to slap. Maybe he didn't care what he slapped. Or maybe he actually wanted, intended, tried to slap my face. Because that's what he slapped. And then we had a big fight about it, and finally, at the end of the fight, I said, 'How would you like it if I slapped your face?' And Craig said, 'I'd like it, go ahead,' and so I did, I slapped his face, not hard, not hard enough for Craig to cry, not hard enough to hurt him, in fact the slap seemed to make him more defiant, more determined to fight, but still, I slapped his face, and then you said, 'I can't believe you just did that,' and I couldn't believe it either, I felt so ashamed, but I didn't say that, instead I said, 'You would have done the same thing,' and then you slapped *my* face. That was the end of that particular fight. It was the only fight where anyone hit anyone else. But sometimes, during the fights after that fight, I actually wished someone would hit someone, because otherwise, the fights never seemed to have any logical endpoint, and without one they seemed like they might go on forever.

"Anyway, I massaged my throat, in the dark. That didn't work, either. If anything, it seemed to make things worse: Instead of relaxing my throat it seemed to make it tenser. I could feel my throat tightening, could feel the chicken burrito expanding, somehow *growing* right there in my throat. There was less and less air coming out, and the whistling was getting quieter and quieter. And then the big lights over the parking lot went off—they were probably on a timer—and the room got darker. So, it was quiet, and dark. The way it gets right before the end of something. And for the first time, it occurred to me that I really might die.

"So I walked to the sink (it was a one-step walk). I turned on the faucet. But remember I didn't have any cups or glasses. So I stuck my head under the tap and drank. Or tried to. But the tap was too long, or the sink was too shallow, and in any case I could barely get my head in there and turn it so that my mouth tipped up toward the faucet, could barely get any water in my mouth, only enough to get my mouth wet, only to get just a taste of how rusty the water was, and definitely not enough to dislodge, or wash down a large piece of chicken burrito that was stuck in my throat, that I was choking on.

"Because I was definitely choking on it, now. Almost no air was coming in and out at all. The whistling sound had stopped altogether and the only sounds I could hear were the traffic out on the interstate. I was still leaning over the sink, and things were bad enough that I sort of left my body, and was hovering over it, examining this body that was bent over the sink, looking like someone about to throw up, and then I had an idea, and so I reentered my body and stuck my finger down my throat so that I would throw up the burrito. For a few seconds I thought this was actually going to work. My body started heaving and I could feel my throat catching and releasing and my eyes started watering and then . . . I could feel the burrito drop, even deeper in my throat, so deep that there's no way I could gag it up. I took my finger out of my mouth. My cell phone was on the counter, next to the sink. I thought about calling you and Craig, but even if I could talk, even if I could make myself heard, what could I say? That our life together was so unhappy that I'd decided, without even telling you first, to rent a terrible apartment, a terrible apartment that had made me happy because neither of you were in it—happy that is, until I started choking on a cold, unmicrowaved microwavable chicken burrito and now I needed you and would you come save me?

"The thought of making that phone call seemed more impossible than dying. And driving to the emergency room, or anywhere, seemed impossible now, too: Just the thought of turning the key in the ignition made me feel exhausted to death. I put the phone down on the counter.

It seemed important to get out of that kitchen area. So I walked into the middle of the living room. I lay down, on the Pergo floor, to die. I lay there for who knows how long, the burrito growing bigger and harder and rounder in my throat, like a giant egg, it really did feel that way, like the chicken in the burrito was going back in time, back before it was large chunks of chicken to be microwaved, back before it was a whole live chicken, back to when it was just an egg, and then I went back in time, too, walked myself, in my mind, back through all the attempts to get the burrito out of my throat, back to when I first started choking on it, back to when I took it out of the plastic wrapper and realized I had no way to microwave it, back to when I bought the thing from the clerk in the Red-E Mart.

"I scrambled to my feet, feeling woozy in the dark, woozy and tired, but also superhumanly energized, the way I guess you are by last chances. I stumbled down the stairs, across parking lot, across the frontage road, into the Red-E Mart. There was only one person in the mart, the clerk, who I knew, from when I'd bought the burrito in there earlier, didn't speak English. I walked up to the counter, gasping, gasping, and tried to make myself understood in sign language. I grabbed my throat with both hands to show that I was choking, but I could see the look of alarm on the clerk's face, could tell that the clerk thought that I was threatening him or something. So I took my hands off my throat and started pounding on my chest, again. That made the clerk look less afraid, but more confused. I then made the traditional of signing of wanting to write something down on a piece of paper, and *that* the clerk understood: He handed me a pen, a piece of paper. I wrote I AM CHOKING!!! But of course the note was in English and clerk couldn't read it. In fact, he seemed more alarmed than ever. I didn't know why until I urgently tapped the note and the clerk raised his hands and I realized that the man thought I was trying to rob him, that the note was a note demanding money, demanding that he open the cash register, the safe. 'No, no!' I said, or tried to, waving my hands wildly, and in doing so I knocked over a display of Slim Jims, knocked them right off the counter, and onto the floor, all except one Slim Jim. I'd never eaten a Slim Jim before. I'd never really even looked at one before, but I looked at it now. Like the name said, it was slim, and also long. It was like the world's slimmest, longest finger, encased in a bright yellow and red wrapper. The wrapper was so bright that it seemed to glow, like something there to guide you in the dark, something there to help you through rough times.

"I grabbed the Slim Jim and without taking it out of its wrapper I jammed it into my mouth and down my throat, jammed it once, twice, and the third time the burrito came loose and I swallowed it. Then I put the Slim Jim back on the counter, thanked the clerk, left the Red-E Mart, crossed the frontage road, got into my car, and drove home to you."

Martin told this story, almost every single word of it, in French.

After I realized that the story was going to be about the time he tried to leave us, I stopped looking at him. I looked at the table, looked at the menu, looked into my wineglass, looked at the ceiling, and finally, having run out of other places to look, I looked at Craig, who was looking at Martin, first in anger and annoyance, of course, but then, as the story went on and on and on, in curiosity, and then amusement, and then wonder. It was like watching Craig go back in time, to the time where the world was there to amaze him and not only to make him look bad. "I've missed you so much," I wanted to say to him, but I didn't want to break the spell. And I didn't want Martin to stop telling the story, either. But he did, of course. He finished the story I've just relayed to you. He'd been leaning back in his chair the entire time, but now he leaned forward, took up his wineglass, took a sip, smiled at me, and Craig, and then said, "Dieu merci pour le Slim Jim!"

Craig laughed and laughed, laughed even harder than when he was a happy kid and laughed all the time. I think it was hearing all that French, all at once, which must have sounded like so much gibberish to him (as far as I know, Craig thought it *was* gibberish: He's never asked what the story was about, if it was about anything, and I've never told him) peppered with and then punctuated by the stupid English words he knew: "Slim Jim," "Red-E Mart." Craig laughed until I thought he was going to hurt himself, laughed until other people in the restaurant were noticing, the way they'd noticed him dropping his menu earlier. I cared then; I didn't care now. I thought, let them notice; let Craig keep laughing forever. Finally, when he'd gotten ahold of himself, Craig said, "Sleem Jeem," in a cartoonish French accent, and then Martin and I laughed, too, laughed almost as hard as Craig had been laughing. This seemed to please him. The waiter came over to take our order, and Craig asked Martin, "What's the French word for hamburger?" Martin told him—"Hamburger"—and Craig laughed at that, too, and then asked the waiter, very politely, if he could please order a hamburger, even though it wasn't on the menu. The waiter said sure, and then Martin and I each ordered whatever it was we ordered, and whatever it was, it was good, and Craig's hamburger was good, too, and all in all I think it was his nicest birthday since he was five years old and we'd first gone to that restaurant and were all so in love with each other.

Two hours later, after we were home, after Craig had said goodnight and we'd said, "Happy birthday, we love you," and he'd said, "Me, too," Martin and I decided to split a beer before we went to bed. He'd taken off his sport coat (he was still wearing the cardigan) and I'd taken off my high heels. We were in the kitchen, with its fully stocked shelves and cabinets and refrigerator and its restaurant quality gas stove and oven and in the middle of the room the island with the barstools around it. I wondered if Martin had been seeing all these things two years earlier while he was lying on the floor of his empty apartment, choking. I'd thought about that apartment a lot over the previous two years. Because I was the one who did all our bills, and balanced our checkbook, and of course I'd noticed that some real estate company I had never heard of had cashed his check, and of course I'd called the company, and of course the manager of the apartment complex had told me that Martin had rented the apartment, and then abandoned it. I never mentioned this to Martin. His near-death experience must have made Martin forget that he'd ever written the check in the first place, because he'd never mentioned it to me, either, not until he'd told the story in Le Miracle. But often, when Martin was either being made miserable by me or Craig, or when he was making us miserable, I wondered why he bothered to come back, why he hadn't just stayed in the apartment. And now that he'd told the story, I also wondered why he'd bothered to get up off the floor on which he had lay down to die. Because in my heart, Martin was already dead. He had died when he'd slapped Craig and when I then slapped Martin. And then he died some more when I found out he'd gotten the apartment, when I realized he didn't have the guts to move out, didn't even have the guts to tell me that he'd rented the apartment in the first place. And now that he'd finally told the story, and seemed to think the story should make me forget all of that, I was sure that Martin was finally and truly dead to me. You're dead, I wanted to say to him. Why don't you just go away forever? Why did you come back? Why didn't you just stay in your apartment? Why didn't you just stay down on that floor in your apartment until you *died*? "Why . . ." I started to ask, in English, but before I could finish Martin kissed me. I kissed him back. We kissed for a long time. We might still be kissing if I hadn't accidentally knocked Martin's glasses off his face and onto the floor. We stopped kissing. Martin leaned over, picked up his glasses, put them back on his face, and I thought the moment was lost, ruined, but then Martin looked at me through his glasses, shrugged—a very Gallic shrug, I remembered it from Toulouse—and said, in French, "I wanted to live."

ONE GOES WHERE ONE IS NEEDED

I say, to the children, in their tinted goggles and their helmets and their puffy jackets and pants and their tiny boots locked into their tiny skis, I say to them, "Ladies and gentlemen, we got him."

The children look at me, look at each other, look back at me. They are five years old. The Hobbit group, so-called. They expect me to teach them how to ski. And I will. But I will also teach them other things. Nation building, for instance.

"I was speaking about Saddam, of course," I say to the children. "We got him, or at least our men and women in uniform, they got him. They got Saddam. We got Saddam. And then the very next day, from behind that podium, I said, 'Ladies and gentlemen, we got him. The tyrant is a prisoner. Now it is time for all Iraqis—Arabs and Kurds, Sunni and Shia, Christians and Turkmen—to build a prosperous, democratic Iraq, at peace with its neighbors."

One of the children raises his hand. He is Ryan, I believe. In this Hobbit group there is a Ryan, there is a Shiloh, there is a Therese, a Chloe, a Hooper, and, strangely, another Hooper. Ryan raises his hand, his blue-mittened hand. I expect he has a question about Turkmen. What one is. Understandable. I had the same question, had asked the same question, just minutes before I gave my famous speech, right before I set about rebuilding Iraq, for the sake of the Turkmen, and for all Iraqis.

"Iraqi Turkmen," I say, "are not directly related to the Turkmen people of Turkmenistan and do not identify as such."

"When do we get our poles?" Ryan wants to know. I don't much like his tone. Nor the camera, attached to the top of his helmet. I know from my experience with the media that the camera is a third eye, that never sleeps, that never sympathizes, that always judges.

"No cameras," I say. And also, "No poles."

How did I, the Provisional Coalition Administrator of postliberation Iraq, become a youth ski instructor here at Okemo Mountain in Ludlow, Vermont?

The desert. The Mountain. The medics. The ski patrols. The tanks. The groomers. The green zone. The black diamonds. The tracer fire. The New Year's Eve fireworks extravaganza. The swirling sand. The swirling snow. The MPs at our security checkpoints. The bouncers in our newly remodeled Loose Boots lounge.

We think the world is big. But there are ways of making it small.

And there is no sense in asking how one begins in one place and ends up in another. One goes where one is needed.

"Paul," Ryan says. We are on the Magic Carpet, I am in front, leading, Ryan right behind me, the other Hobbits behind him. It is minus two degrees Fahrenheit, if one does not count the windchill (I do not count the windchill), but the sun is powerful and the snow has been organized by our industry-best groomers into miles and miles of sweet corduroy. "Paul," Ryan says again, and the tip of one of his skis taps the heel of my boot. I don't answer. As I've already told him, have already told the entire hobbit group, that while my name is Paul, I would strongly prefer that they called me "Ambassador" or "Viceroy." Because these are titles I've earned. It's important, as Hobbits, that they understand this, if they are ever to advance to the next level of group lessons. Where they will be Grizzlies.

Hobbits. Grizzlies. I've suggested to the Big Ed, the head of our ski school, that it would make more sense if the advanced group were named, say, the Elves, or the beginning group the Cubs. But Big Ed, who has a red nose that suggests alcoholism, and a wild ill-kempt beard that suggests a lack of self-respect, says that for forty years it has been Hobbits and Grizzlies and people have gotten used to Hobbits and Grizzlies and while Hobbits and Grizzlies might not be perfect, it would create more problems than it's worth if suddenly there's something other than Hobbits and Grizzles.

This was the kind of thinking that I fought in Iraq, and this is the kind of thinking I am still fighting at Okemo.

"*Paul*," Ryan says, again, and I turn to remind him of my preferred nomenclature, and I see that he is sprawled on the Magic Carpet, one ski dragging on the snow, and the other tucked underneath. It looks painful. But Ryan is grinning, and I suspect he's fallen on purpose, to see what I will do, to see if I will help him up, to see what kind of ski instructor I really am.

There is Patrick, twenty-five years old, white, dreadlocks, no hat. He has not bothered to learn any of his students' names. They are all, each of them, "little dude." His method is to place a harness on his students, and attach a leash to the harness, and then to ski behind his students, holding them up by the leash. "Shreddin', little dude!" he says, to each of them. But I think that even they know that they are not shredding. They are puppets. Puppets don't shred.

There are the twins, Emma and Rachel. Twenty years old, also white, identical, except for their helmets (pink and canary yellow, respectively). They have learned their students' names. They know where they're from. They know their preferred snacks. That is to their credit. You must know your people in order to get them to follow you. But the twins, they do not get their students to follow them. They hold their Hobbits between their legs as they traverse the bunny slope. There is something disturbing about this. Something unnatural. Four skis where there should be two.

There is Allyson, with a "y." White. Braces. Does not believe in goggles. She squints in the sun like Saddam when we first extracted him from his lair. She is a teenager. New to driving. She talks about her license, incessantly. The unfair restrictions on it. She's not allowed to drive with friends or anything. Although I think she drives with friends anyway. Her way is not the leash or the straddle. She lets her students ski. But she yells at them. She yells at them to "Pizza! Pizza!" This refers to the triangular pizza slice shape she wishes them to make with their skis. But what of the personal pizza? That is the kind of pizza these children are used to. "Pizza! Pizza!" Allyson yells at them, and they are baffled. Better not to tell them anything at all.

There is Gareth, white, Australian, early thirties, who is the Hobbit snowboard instructor. I will not speak of him or his method. The snowboard is an abomination. If this were my mountain, I would ban snowboarders, strip them of their rights, revoke their season passes.

Me? I am seventy-six years old, white (unlike in the desert, we are all white here on the mountain). My method? I deny my students their poles. I do not allow them to extend their arms for balance. Instead, I make them stick their hands in their parka pockets. I demand that they close their eyes. I take away everything they have always relied upon, everything they think they need to function, to thrive, to move forward. And then I let them ski.

What do I see when I see Iraq? I see Iraq. The country we built. The country we rebuilt. Out of chaos, we made order. Out of autocracy, we made democracy.

What don't I see when I see Iraq? What other people see.

"Murderer!" a snowboarder screams, at me, through her balaclava, as she swooshes past me and toward our brand-new highspeed quad.

In front of me: bodies. Hooper and the other Hooper have collided, and their skis have gotten tangled with one another and while still standing, are stuck in what seems like an unlockable embrace: The larger of the Hoopers is laughing, and the littler Hooper is crying, in each other's faces. Chloe is lying, back-down, where she has fallen, not ten feet from the top of the bunny hill, sucking on her mitten. Therese has face-planted, and is screaming into the packed powder for her mother. Your mother can't hear you, Therese, I want to say. Your mother is spending the morning in our four-season spa. And Shiloh: Shiloh appears to have already abandoned us, and joined another group lesson. There he is, between Rachel's legs, where he is learning not how to ski, but how to be held. "I got him!" Rachel shouts to me, and waves, with her right hand, and when she does Shiloh lists to the right, and a look of terror washes over his face, and then Rachel puts her right hand back on him, and Shiloh is steadied, and looks reassured, but he has not learned to ski, he has not learned anything except that Rachel can reassure him. But what happens when Rachel is gone? What happens when the season ends and Rachel resumes her position as a bike technician in Burlington? What will Shiloh do then?

And Ryan? He is already at the bottom of the slope, where he's receiving high fives from Patrick. "Little dude!" I hear Patrick say to the boy. And then, to me, "He's a pro!" Perhaps. But then, I have reasons to distrust pros.

In Iraq the pros were Baathists. They were Saddam's people. They were his pros. And I fired all of them. I got rid of the judges, the generals, the politicians. I got rid of the doctors, the teachers, the architects. I got rid of everyone who knew what they were doing. This was what I told them, as they came to my office, in the Republican Palace, one by one, to be fired: You *knew* what you were *doing*. They nodded, as though this said something positive about their future in the new Iraq. Goodbye, I said. See you soon, they said. And then I never saw any of them again.

After I finished firing all of them, I stepped out of my office, out of the Republican Palace, out into Baghdad, out into the Green Zone in Baghdad. The sky was a riot of orange and blue. I heard the sound of industry: trucks, tanks, shouting, orders being delivered and followed. Gunfire in the distance. There was a breeze, a gentle one. I let it ruffle my hair, let it blow dirt and litter over my Timberlands. Somewhere there was music playing—a native tune, I thought, something eerie and otherworldly. But then I recognized it: Michael Jackson's "Thriller." I followed the song, to one of our tents. I opened the flap and inside saw four of our women in uniform. Each of them was drinking something out of a red Solo cup. I assumed it was alcohol. On their faces, glassy eyes and crooked smiles and war paint. They were all sitting on folding camping chairs at one end of the tent. On the other were two men, both Iraqis. One was a short man, wearing a fedora, and a trench coat that pooled at his ankles. He may have very well been a boy, and not a man—I couldn't see his face clearly, because of the fedora. He had his finger on a button of a portable stereo. When he saw me enter the tent, he pushed pause, and suddenly there was no more "Thriller." The short man in the fedora then looked up at his countryman. His countryman was naked, except for his leopard-skin briefs, his calf-high yellow leather boots. His hair was deep black and hung past his shoulders, and he looked for all the world like a professional wrestler. But he was not a professional wrestler. He was a stripper. A male stripper. With both hands he gripped a floor lamp. This was clearly his stripper's pole. He was improvising. He was making do. I admired that. But the pole, which was in reality the lamp, was awfully short. It came up to his chest and was clearly unsuitable for a man of his size, with his needs. The scene made me sad, for a second, and then after that resolved, as I came face to face with another example of the enormity of my task. Meanwhile, the stripper must have recognized me as the man in charge, a man who could get things done. He said, "I must require a much taller lamp."

"Are you a Baathist?" I asked him.

He assured me he was not.

And it was difficult. It was not a nation, at that time, with a surplus of lamps, of any size. But eventually, as with the people of Iraq as a whole, I got the man what he needed: I got him a much taller lamp.

I say to the Hoopers, "I think we Americans, of all people, understand the importance of a good, legal, constitutional framework as the basis of political life." They are trying to disentangle themselves, their skis, and I mean for this to be encouragement. But it doesn't seem to have the desired effect: One Hooper, the larger one, blames the littler one for their joint failure, and pushes him, in the chest, and in doing so, the littler Hooper falls backward, onto the snow, dragging the larger Hooper down with him. Where the pushing evolves into wrestling, which, with skis attached to their feet, has the potential to be more hazardous than ordinary boyish wrestling. "I think the Iraqi people showed extraordinary patience and courage," I tell them. And I'm about to tell them more about the Iraq people's extraordinary patience and courage when I notice, at the bottom of the hill, Ryan talking with Big Ed, the head of the ski school. Big Ed is nodding, nodding, and then he looks in my direction. At me. And what does he see? What he should see is a ski instructor who is allowing his students to learn from their mistakes. But what he might see is a grown man allowing two five-year-old boys to assault each other. Big Ed glances back at Ryan, nods some more, then heads back into the lodge. Ryan looks at me, waves, and then proceeds to the Magic Carpet. I told all my students that they are not allowed to get on the Magic Carpet by themselves. That we will do so as a group, or not at all. But there is Ryan, getting on the Magic Carpet by himself. "But we dominate the scene," I tell the Hoopers, one of whom is crying, the other swearing, I can't tell which, because I'm not looking at them. I'm looking at Ryan, moving toward me, inexorably, on the Magic Carpet. His grin, and his tiny white baby teeth, they glitter in the sun. "And we will," I say, "continue to impose our will."

It was said that I said that we should shoot the looters. The Iraqi looters who were stealing computers, television sets, radios, clothes, food, nails, wood, everything. And it was said that I said we should shoot them. But I did not say that. I said that we should have the *right* to shoot them. I said that we should be *allowed* to shoot them. But the generals, my own generals, said that our military code of conduct did not allow our men and women in uniform to shoot someone just because he was, say, stealing a computer. Now you see what I was up against. And so I asked the generals, But what if a looter were stealing a nuclear weapon? Should we be allowed to shoot the looter if he were stealing a nuclear weapon? Wait, the generals said, are there nuclear weapons in Iraq? No, I said. But what if there were?

Six of us, around a fire, the flames rising skyward out of a scorched metal trashcan. This was not Baghdad, but Okemo. Wednesday, December sixteenth, two months before the Hobbit group lesson with Ryan, et al., the night before the first day of the winter season. The night before my first day as a ski instructor. Patrick, the twins, Allyson,

Gareth. We were passing around a bottle of Fireball. This was outside the Bunkhouse, the long, low slung gray clapboard building where all the ski instructors live. It was snowing, the sky was thick with it; it had already covered the trees and the ground. White on white, in the darkness. Way above us, on the mountain, the lights of the groomers were making their serpentine way down the Headwall. It might have been the Fireball, or might have been the Bob Marley, playing on Patrick's cell phone, telling us that every little thing was going to be all right, but I had the strong feeling, as I'd had the strong feeling in Iraq, that every little thing really was going to be all right. Maybe even better than just all right. The bottle came to me again, and I raised it to toast my new, young fellow ski instructors, and then took a swig from the bottle, and felt the happy burn in my mouth, and throat, and then I passed the bottle to Patrick, who raised the bottle to toast me in return. And I will not lie: That felt good, being toasted. It had not happened in a very long time. It certainly had not happened in Iraq. And it made me feel very close to Patrick, like I could ask him things that I was not normally inclined to ask. And so I asked him, "Can I touch your hair?"

Patrick had already been fondling—Patrick, I've learned since then, is always fondling—one of the ropey strands of his dreadlocks. "Have at it, dude," he said, and then dipped his head and extended his dread in my direction. I took off my right glove and touched his hair. It felt cold, hard, but also gritty. After touching it, I fought off the strong urge to wipe my hand on my pants. Because I thought that would be impolite, especially given that Patrick had so kindly consented to let me touch his hair in the first place. Instead, I released the dread and said, "Cool." That word felt strange in my mouth, and I wondered if it sounded strange, too, because one of the twins laughed (I could not tell which—neither of them were wearing their telltale helmets) and the other one punched her in the arm, silencing her. For a moment, everyone was quiet—no sound at all except the crackle of the fire and the whoosh of the wind through the tall pines—and I had the thought (and it was true that I'd had this thought before) that I was exactly where I was supposed to be. And then Patrick, once again fondling his dread, asked me, "How many people did you kill?"

"What?" I said. Although of course I knew what. And although I hadn't told the other instructors who I was, and where I had been before Okemo, I should have known that they would have known. When you're someone like me, you can't get away from people knowing who you were, or thinking they know who you are.

"How many people did you kill in Iraq?" Patrick said.

"I didn't kill anyone in Iraq," I said. "I didn't kill anyone anywhere."

"You mean not personally."

"Correct," I said.

"But you were in charge," Patrick said. "People died when you were in charge."

I knew what Patrick wanted me to say. I knew what they all wanted me to say: "I know. I'm sorry." Even the Fireball wanted me to say it: I could feel it working at the words in my throat, in my mouth, loosening them, so they could finally come pouring out. But if they were to come out, then what else would I have inside me? What else would be left?

"People also died before I was in charge," I said, as coolly as possible. "And they've been dying since, too." I could hear one of the twins suck in her breath, and I noticed that the other twin did not punch her in the arm this time. Patrick nodded, like he'd heard what he wanted, or expected, to hear. He then used his sleeve to wipe the mouth of the bottle, took a drink from it, and then passed it to the next person.

We are now down to four. We have lost the littler Hooper. He is back in the Hobbit Hole, eating Snack, although it is not yet time for Snack. There are forty-five minutes until Snack. But the littler Hooper demanded Snack, through his tears, and so I let him go to Snack. "But how will you get there?" I asked him. Rhetorically. Because I knew how. The littler Hooper wiped his nose with his sleeve, took off his skis, and dragging them behind him, like they were the legs of a missing body, walked down the bunny slope, in his massive boots, heel to toe, heel to toe. Halfway down he staggered, slipped, fell backward, hard, his helmeted head striking one of his skis, the other one shooting down the slope, toward the lodge, where it disappeared underneath the wooden access ramp. "How will your parents get back their security deposit?" I called to him. Again, rhetorically. Because I knew his parents would not be getting back their security deposit. The littler Hooper hit the snow with both fists, and we all could all hear his weeping. He sat up, then stood up, reached back to grab his remaining ski, and once again lost his balance, and fell, hard, flinging the ski forward, and we all watched as it, too, shot down the slope and disappeared under the ramp. The rest of the Hobbit Group laughed. I let them. I hoped this was a valuable lesson for the littler Hooper. Even the easy way out is hard.

"Even the easy way out is hard," I told the rest of the Hobbits, and they nodded, all of them, except for Ryan, who was once again on his way down the slope. He side-stopped inches away from the littler Hooper, spraying him with snow. Another valuable lesson, I thought, begrudgingly. But then Ryan stuck out his hand, and the smaller Hooper grabbed it, and Ryan hoisted him to his feet, brushed the snow off the littler Hooper's helmet, patted the littler Hooper on his back, seemed to whisper some kind of encouragement in the littler Hooper's ear, then sent the littler Hooper on his way to the Hobbit Hole. Then Ryan turned in our direction and herringboned his way up the slope, moving faster than even the Magic Carpet. In seconds he was standing next to us. He wasn't even breathing hard. "Hey Paul," he said. I waited for him to say something else. He didn't say something else. But even his silence felt like a judgment.

I had a reputation, unfounded. That, as an Ambassador, as a Viceroy, I was remote. That I wasn't sufficiently involved. Well, let me tell you a story. The last Friday of every other month, in the Republican Palace, in the Green Zone, I sat behind a table and received, one by one, a long line of Iraqis who came with questions and complaints. A man whose house had been run over by a tank. A woman, a government employee, who wanted to know about her salary. A girl who lost her parents and wanted to know if I knew where they were. A boy who had lost an arm and who wanted me to help him get a new one. I listened, patiently, carefully, wrote down their questions and complaints, no matter how big, no matter how small. And when they were through, I asked each person for their phone number. And each person said something to the effect of, "I have no phone number. The phone system of Iraq has been destroyed." But still, I was not discouraged, still I persisted, still I remained involved. And when it was the next person's turn, I wrote down their questions and complaints, and then I asked, "Phone number?" hoping, expecting, that eventually, I would get the right answer.

"We've had complaints," Big Ed says. He's joined us on the bunny slope. Where we've remained. Where some of us have remained. Therese has defected to Patrick's group, has already gone down the hill, guided by Patrick and his rope and is in the Hobbit Hole, also enjoying Snack. Ryan, meanwhile, is agitating to try a Blue. He says, "Paul, I'm so ready for a Blue." But he is not so ready for a Blue. He is not even so ready for a Green. Chloe and the larger Hooper simply stand there, dazed, wobbly on their skis. They've been on the Bunny Slope for two hours and twenty-three minutes and have moved ten feet.

"We've had complaints," Big Ed says. Big Ed isn't wearing skis. I've not seen Big Ed wear skis once during my six weeks at Okemo. What kind of head of ski school doesn't wear skis? This is why I wore work boots in Iraq. To show that I was prepared to build, and so to inspire the others who would actually then do the building.

"Complaints from whom?" I ask. Ryan is to my left. Big Ed's bloodshot eyes cut to Ryan, for a second, for less than a second, then back to me.

"Never mind who," Big Ed says. But I think I know who. "Last chance," Big Ed says. Because there have been complaints before. Because there have been other Ryans before this Ryan. I don't just mean at Okemo; I also mean in Iraq, where the generals ended up being Ryans and our men and women in uniform ended up being Ryans, and the Arabs and Kurds, Sunni and Shia, Christians and even the Turkmen ended up being Ryans. All of them, people who thought they knew better, until they were forced to confront the obvious truth, which was that they did not know better, which was when they blamed me for not teaching them, or allowing them, to know better. If, that is, they were still around to do the blaming.

"I need to go to the bathroom," the larger Hooper says—not to me, but to Big Ed. I don't think that the larger Hooper does need to use the bathroom—it's the first I've heard of it—but Big Ed just nods, says, "Sure thing, buddy. Can you pizza?" To my surprise, the larger Hooper says, "Yup," and then pizzas his way to the lodge, Big Ed rumbling behind him. I watch the larger Hooper go, with mixed feelings. I learned, in Iraq, and now in Okemo, that some departures are a sorrow, and also a relief. You're gone before I even knew you, larger Hooper, I think, but then, that spares us another kind of departure, a different sort of sorrow.

"Wow," Ryan says, still to my right. "Where'd Hooper learn to pizza like that?" I don't say anything, but I can hear the "gee whiz" in his voice. The "gee whiz" is insincere. Because Ryan knows he knows where. "I bet he was watching Allyson, when he should have been paying attention to you." He pauses again. *Don't*, I say, to Ryan, in my head. *Do not*. But this time it's my turn to speak, or at least think, insincerely. Because saying *do* when you should say *don't* is another kind of relief. "I hear Allyson is the best ski instructor," Ryan says, and I turn to look at him. Those white teeth again, on display, the sun bouncing off them like they're tiny shards of glass. "No offense," he adds.

I nod to let him know that I'm not offended, and then I say, "You know, I think you are ready for that Blue." I don't need to tell him twice. Off Ryan skis, toward the high-speed quad, and then it is just me and Chloe.

My last day in Iraq. A year after I'd first arrived. There was a ceremony, where I'd handed over control of Iraq to the interim Iraqi government. It was a wonderful occasion that, unfortunately, had to be held in a secret location. Because of security concerns. You could argue that our not holding this ceremony in public was a sign of our failure. You could also argue that we did not accomplish all, or most, or any, of what we'd set out to do. But then, we'd set out to do a lot.

After the ceremony, we headed to the airfield. Where the transport plane waited for us. We told everyone that we were taking the transport plane to Germany. But we were not going to take the transport plane. We were going to take a much smaller, less obvious plane. Again, for security reasons. But right before I got on the plane and turned to take one last look at Iraq, I saw a small group of protestors, on the far side of the cyclone fence. "No to America!" they chanted. But also, "No to Saddam!" Some Ambassadors, some Viceroys, would have felt defeated by that. But I felt heartened. True, we had caused these Iraqis to hate us, but in doing so, at least we'd made them remember to keep hating the person they'd hated before they started hating us, too. This is no victory, I've been told, but only by people who don't know that there are many different kinds of victories.

Twenty minutes later, I hear shouting. The ski patrol, barking into their walkie-talkies, calling for a stretcher, a neck brace. A kid, a boy, has had an accident. On Sidewinder, which is a Blue, an especially gnarly one. Unfortunate. But as all the signs inform you before you get on the lifts, it's important that you know your limitations.

"OK, Chloe," I say. I pat her on the helmet, then ski backward down to the bottom of the bunny slope. It is the end of the group lesson. Everyone is watching: the other groups, most of my former Hobbits, Big Ed, Chloe's parents. I nod at her, and then Chloe begins to ski. Truly ski. In her own way, not guided by ropes or human hands or instructions or metaphor or analogy. It is not perfect, perhaps. It is not even pretty. Twenty feet from the bottom, Chloe wobbles, windmills her arms, lurches backward, and then falls forward, sliding face first down the rest of the mountain. A gasp and then a hush over the bunny slope. Chloe comes to a stop just inches from my skis. Looks up at me. Her chin is bleeding, dripping into the snow. She opens her mouth, and there is a gap, two front teeth missing, and I can't honestly say that they were missing before she fell. It is grisly. But it is beautiful. Because you have to see the grisly things that you made as beautiful or you will die, inside, and if you are dead inside then you are no different, no better, than the people who have died outside. A heady concept. One I don't expect to Chloe to understand, so I don't explain it to her. Instead, I bend down, get Chloe to her feet, wipe the snow off her jacket, the blood off her chin, the tears from her cheeks. Her eyes are flickering everywhere—maybe she's looking for her parents, maybe she's in shock. "Chloe," I say, firmly, and then I wait until she looks me in the eyes, so that she understands what has just happened, understands the enormity of it. Finally she does, she looks me in the eyes, and I say to her, "We did it."

CUSTOMS AND ALTERATIONS

Finally, fifteen months after he died, I get my son's death certificate in the mail. There it is: the manner of his death, and the time, and the date, and the place, and also his name. It's misspelled. Both his first and his last name are misspelled. His middle name they got right.

*

"I like the name, you like the name, we both like the name. But you just know people are going to take the "e" off the end of his last name and put it on his first. So don't act all surprised and pissed off when it happens."

This was said by Emelie, my ex-wife. Whose name is also often misspelled.

*

"What did I tell you?" texts Emelie, in response to my texting her that they spelled our son's name wrong on his death certificate.

"I'm at work," texts Emelie, in response to my texting her, asking what we should do about it.

*

Emelie is the Director of The Center of Teaching and Learning.

A School is what we used to call a Center for Teaching and Learning, and a Principal is what we used to call a Director.

*

Me, I used to be a journalist. But now I write lists. Last month I wrote Top Eight Cities for Book Nerds. Last week I wrote Four Signs You Need to Clean Out Your Refrigerator. Next week I'll write Seven Ways for Bald Men to Repurpose Their Combs.

*

I say "I used to be journalist." But the company I'm employed by also owns the newspaper where I used to be a journalist. And in fact my boss now was my editor then, and he is in fact still the editor of the newspaper, although he no longer calls the newspaper the newspaper.

The Traditional Media Outlet is what he now calls what we used to call the newspaper.

*

"Two reasons," my editor said, when I asked him why he'd decided I was no longer going to be a journalist for the Traditional Media Outlet but was instead going to write lists for the website that was owned by the holding company that also owned the Traditional Media Outlet. "First, ever since your son died your heart just doesn't seem in it anymore."

He left unsaid what was nevertheless perfectly clear: that the people who write lists for a living are people whose hearts just aren't in it anymore.

"And what's the second reason?" I wanted to know.

"I'm in a bind," my editor said. "My list guy was just shot to death. And so was his dog."

"Oh my God," I said, but my editor told me not to worry, their murders had nothing to do with his list guy's lists.

*

There's a letter that comes with the death certificate. On it, there's a number for me to call if I have any complaints or suggestions. But when I call the number the automated voice tells me that they are no longer taking complaints or suggestions over the phone. "Please come visit us at our main office," the voice tells me, without telling me where their main office is.

*

This—the certificate opening, the phone calling, the texting—is happening in my apartment. The apartment is new, to me. It's on the second floor of a three-story brick building. On the second and third floors of the building are apartments like mine, I guess, although I haven't seen any except the one I'm in. On the first floor are businesses—a coffee shop, a wig store, and, right below my apartment, a place that, according to the lettering on their awning, does "Customs and Alterations." Sometimes, when it's very quiet, like right now, I can hear the sewing machines jittering down there like thoughts in the too-early morning.

*

I find the address of the main office. A twenty-minute walk from my apartment. It's a beautiful day out there! Although about halfway to the main office I come across a downed electrical wire, writhing and sparking and looking like a dangerous living thing. One of the poles the wire had been attached to is lying on top of the hood of a car. And into the back of that car is the accordioned front of another car.

I'm on one side of the wire. On the other side are two men. One of them gestures at the wire, and then he gestures at the man next to him. That man raises his hands, palms out, the universal sign for "Hey, not my fault, pal." The men start yelling at each other: They have gone from gesturing and pointing to yelling just like that. After a minute of this yelling, one of the men decides yelling isn't good enough anymore: He pushes the other man, hard, and that man staggers and almost falls. If he'd fallen, he'd have fallen on the wire, which seems to hiss and leap toward him in anticipation.

I decide to turn around and take an alternate route to the main office, but before I do, I hear the one man say, "You're going to regret that" to the other man, who then says, in so many words, that he highly doubts it.

*

"If that plane leaves the ground and you're not with him, you'll regret it. Maybe not today. Maybe not tomorrow, but soon, and for the rest of your life."

Is number six on my Top Ten Lines from Classic Movies You'll Never Forget.

Although that one line is in fact three lines. Dumbass.

Wrote one helpful reader.

*

"You're not going to believe what I saw on the way over here," says the woman behind me in line.

"Two men fighting next to a downed electrical wire," I say to the woman.

"Boom!" the woman says to me. Which apparently is what one man said to the other man after he managed to throw the other man directly onto the wire.

*

And which man threw which man?

The woman tells me, and I say, "Huh, I would have guessed the other way around."

*

Half an hour later I make it to the front of the line.

"Please don't get in line unless you have these documents," says the sign at the front of the line.

*

"Wire down across Elm and Oak. Emergency vehicles on scene. Injuries reported. Please find alternate route," says an alert on my phone.

*

My alternate route back to my apartment takes me past a hospital. It's the hospital where my son died.

*

Was he brave? No, none of us were brave.

*

Back in my apartment I can't find all the documents. In a panic I go through the documents I brought with me to the main office and discover that I'd already had all the documents.

*

I've been seeing a therapist. The last time I saw her she said that when I feel the rage coming on, I should make an animal noise. What kind of animal? I asked, and the therapist said it didn't matter which kind, as long as it was it an animal I could imagine being very angry and making a very angry noise. But why? I wanted to know. My therapist said that either making the noise would drive away the feeling of rage, or making the noise would cause me to feel so stupid that I wouldn't want to feel the rage so that I wouldn't have to make the noise again.

I make the noise. I yell as loud as I can, for as long as I can, until someone in Customs and Alterations bangs on their ceiling to tell me to stop. I stop. But I don't feel any different than before I'd started yelling. My therapist said that if the yelling didn't work, I should call her. I call her, and tell her about the yelling, and also what led to it. Then I wait to hear her response. It's a long time coming. Downstairs I can hear the sewing machines talking to each other.

"OK, folks," she finally says. I've noticed she has this habit of saying "folks" as though she's talking to multiple people, and not just me. "What's the opposite of rage?"

"Death," I say.

"No," the therapist says. "Death is the opposite of life."

"I thought death is a part of life," I say. Because that was what people said after my son died, and in fact my therapist was one of those people. It was supposed to be comforting. But how?

"Let's try again, folks," my therapist says. "What do *you* think would make the rage go away?"

"If my son's name were spelled correctly on his death certificate."

"And what if it doesn't?" she asks.

Now, it's my turn to make her wait for a response. I make her wait and wait and wait until finally she says, "You think that getting your son's name spelled correctly on his death certificate will somehow make up for the fact that your son died, and you couldn't or didn't do anything about it."

"Well, yeah," I say, and then I hang up.

*

There are four rooms in my apartment: the living room, the kitchen, the bedroom, and the bathroom. In the living room there is a fist-sized hole in the wall. And over that hole there is a calendar: Scenes of America. Snowcapped mountains. Rushing rivers. Sun-dappled beaches. Mist-shrouded lighthouses. No people.

*

"No one counts the bathroom as one of the rooms," said Emelie after I told her I had moved into a four-room apartment. "The bathroom is a whole separate category of room."

*

Emelie lives in her own apartment on the other side of the neighborhood, in a new building called the Citizen.

"Why is it called the Citizen?" I asked her, and she said there was no particular reason. "It's just a name, Silas."

Silas being just my name.

*

"Poor, poor Silas," my father used to say to me when he thought I was feeling sorry for myself.

He would say that not in his own voice, but in a baby voice.

"Poo-wah, poo-wah Siwas," is what he actually would say.

This went on throughout my childhood until at age sixteen I finally told him, "It really pisses me off when you say that."

"God, what took you so long?" my father wanted to know.

*

"My throat hurts," my son said. He'd just come home from school, and was gulping, and wincing.

"I'm sure it's nothing," I reassured him.

"My throat *really hurts*," he told me.

"You poor guy," I said, and even though I did not say this in a baby voice, my son looked at me, startled, as though he could hear, as I was hearing, my father's voice in my own.

*

Four Completely Safe Sleeping Pills to Help Get You Through the Night.

Was the title of another one of my lists.

"Sleeping pill" is not a proper scientific or pharmaceutical term. "Hypnotic" is more accurate. As is "sedative." And no "hypnotic" or "sedative" is completely safe, not even if you call them "sleeping pills."

Wrote another helpful reader.

*

I take another alternate route back to the main office, past the dog park, which is on fire.

*

This time there's no line to get into the main office. But there is a typed note on the door that reads: Due to the high volume of walk-in traffic, we're as of immediately only taking complaints and suggestions over the phone.

*

"Go fuck yourself" is a suggestion handwritten on the typed note.

*

"Do you ever think about him?" Emelie asked me, after our son died, but before we got divorced, and moved into our separate apartments.

"Do *you* ever think about him?" I asked back.

"Of course I think about him," she said. "All the time. Every minute of the freaking day."

Then, she waited.

I did not want to admit the truth. Which was that I did not think about him. Because when I thought about him, all I could think, all I could remember, was he was sick, and then he went into the hospital, and then he died.

"Same," is what I finally said.

*

Although I do suddenly now recall that he liked to pick his nose until it was bloody. Not caring who saw it or what they said about it. Always while watching television.

*

I don't go back to my apartment. Instead, I stand right outside the main office and dial the number for the main office.

I don't expect a human to answer the phone, not right away; I expect to have to go down the Habitrail of voice commands and I'm sorry I didn't hear thats and then the piano music that calms you, supposedly, while you're made to wait for a very long time before you're connected to the right person who can help you. But no, I get a human straight away. Her name is Susan. She asks how she can help me.

"You misspelled my son's name on his death certificate," I tell her.

"It does happen," she says. "And for that we apologize." Then, she hangs up.

*

I belong to the neighborhood internet chat room, Next Door. In it, you can read about the goings on in the neighborhood. Most of the goings on are cars that have been broken into. The break-ins are isolated incidents, according to some neighbors. But according to other neighbors they are clear evidence of the neighborhood's and probably the whole entire world's swift decline.

*

I call Emelie at the Center for Learning and Teaching.

“Her instructions are that she’s not to be disturbed,” says Emelie’s administrative assistant.

“Yes,” says Emelie’s administrative assistant, when I ask her whether Emelie doesn’t want to be disturbed by anyone, or just me.

*

Only once did Emelie go with me to see the therapist.

“What do you think of when you look at Silas?” asked the therapist of Emilie.

“I think of him getting raped in prison,” said Emelie. “Which would be terrible,” she quickly added.

But she’d said the first thing like she’d really meant it, and the second thing like it was something she was supposed to say, and not long after that we moved out of our house, and into our new apartments.

*

When he was excited about something my son would clench his fists and shake—no, *vibrate*—with happiness. That’s another thing I suddenly remember about him.

For instance, when he was eight, he was relentless in his campaign to convince us that it was in our family’s collective best interest to get him a dog, and if not a dog, then a turtle, a budgie, a meercat, a hedgehog, a hairless guinea pig, some fish, a ferret.

Finally, we got a kitten. When I brought home the kitten, my son clenched his fists and *vibrated* with happiness. The shaking was so violent I had to wait for it to stop before handing him the kitten.

*

Five Dog Parks You and Your Pooch Will Love was on my list of possible future lists.

*

Did Emelie and I ever love each other? Well, yeah. Are you saying we still don’t?

*

I call the main office again. This time I am made to follow the voice commands, and then I am forced to repeat myself, and then I'm told to please wait and enjoy the music. Rage, rage. First, after my son's death, I was told the rage was healthy, and normal. After a while, I was told it was still normal, but not especially productive. And a while after that, I was told that it was counterproductive, self-destructive, and destructive to other people. After that, people stopped telling me what it was.

*

According to someone on Next Door, the dog park fire might be connected to the wire being down between Oak and Elm. But then, according to someone else on Next Door, it might not be connected at all.

*

The next morning our son's sore throat was worse. And now he had a fever.

"I think we should take him to the pediatrician," Emelie said.

"Are we both going to take him?" I asked.

"Why would we both take him?" she asked.

"I don't know," I said. "But you said that *we* should take him."

This conversation, which was now an argument, was being conducted over the phone.

Emelie was at work. I was at home. Because while Emelie had to work from work, I could—even though I was still at this point a journalist and not a list-maker—occasionally work from home if I needed to. Although it wasn't ideal.

And by arguing about that "we," I was reminding her of that fact.

"I can take him to the pediatrician," she finally said.

"No," I said. "I'll do it. You're at work."

*

What would I do differently?

Almost everything.

*

"Doesn't it just feel like everything has gone to shit?" someone writes on Next Door.

This promptly gets him banned from Next Door.

"You can't talk like that in here," writes whoever is in charge of deciding who can talk like what in here.

*

This is all happening in a city, a medium-sized one. But I grew up in the country, in a white house with black shutters, and a gravel driveway with a green strip of grass down the middle, halfway up the long hill from the town to the mountains. The farms around us had wells, but we were hooked into the town's water source. My father used to always say, "We have *town* water," although I don't remember why he would say this, or to whom, or why they would have cared. It occurs to me now that we might have been getting *town* water illegally.

Occasionally, after a midwinter thaw and then a freeze, something would go wrong with the town water, and rather than call the town, my father would trudge up the hill, holding a large wrench, to where there was a grate on the side of the road. He would remove the grate and descend into the hole, which was filled with icy water. At the bottom of the icy water was a pipe that connected to other pipes, including our pipe. I don't know what my father would do down there—loosen or tighten something, I guess—but eventually he'd emerge from the hole, wet, and shaking, with bright red cheeks and deep blue lips. I'd take the wrench and mallet and we'd walk home. Home, the water would be working again, and while my father took a hot bath I would walk around in a catatonic way, as though preparing myself for tragedy. I just knew that my father was going to die from going down into that hole, that town water would kill him, but no, it was prostate cancer that ended up getting him.

*

But when my son was unhappy, when he was angry, with me, with himself, or even when he was just a little bit frustrated, he would yell, "I'm going to choke myself to death!" And then he would put his hands around his throat and choke himself.

*

Emelie saw my apartment only once. She'd come over to bring me a lamp she didn't need in her new apartment, a lamp from our old house. The walls were bare—no hole yet, and so no calendar needed to cover it. No desk. No end table. No coffee table. No kitchen table. No television. Just a couch placed in the middle of the living room, and a mattress on the floor in the bedroom.

Emelie walked from room to room, appraising. She is a small woman but a heavy walker who wears clunky big-heeled boots. Downstairs at Customs and Alterations, the sewing machines paused just long enough for someone to pound on the ceiling to tell us to keep it down before starting up again. The sound of the machines, once they get going, are like that of a tiny train that just keeps on accelerating and never fades into the distance.

Emelie gave the floor both middle fingers and then turned to leave. I was standing between her and the door. On her way out, walking lightly, on her toes, she stopped and patted me on the cheek.

"Congratulations, Silas," she said. "You picked the perfect place to lose your mind."

*

Someone finally answers. It's not Susan. It's a man. Horace. He asks how I can help him.

"Do you mean, how *you* can help *me*?"

There's a pause. "What'd I say?" Horace wants to know. I tell him. "Shit," Horace says, and then sighs and says, "I've been doing that." Horace wants to know if he can try again, and I say sure, and he does and gets it right this time.

"Someone," I tell him, "a woman named Susan, she hung up on me when I called earlier."

"You were probably just disconnected," Horace says.

"I was hung up on," I repeat. "That's a kind of disconnection."

"You were probably accidentally disconnected," Horace says.

"Do you know Susan?" I ask.

"Which one's Susan?" Horace asks—not me, I don't think. I think he's talking to someone else in the room he's in. I picture a large room with movable dividers and lots of people sitting at desks and wearing headsets. There's a faint voice in the background that says something to Horace and then I hear Horace saying, clearly, to me, "Oh yeah, I know Susan."

"Is she the kind of person who would hang up on a . . ." But then I struggle to know what to call myself. Am I client? A customer? A citizen? Someone seeking justice? Someone seeking satisfaction? Someone seeking compensation? Someone seeking a minor change? Someone seeking a major change? Someone seeking . . .

"I'd like to take this opportunity," Horace interrupts, "to ask you to please pardon my French."

"What?"

"Earlier I said 'shit,'" Horace says, and again I hear a faint voice in the background and Horace laughs ruefully and says, "And there, I said it again."

"I didn't even notice," I say, although I did notice.

"Is there anything else I can help you with?" Horace asks.

"You haven't helped me with anything yet," I point out. Immediately, I can feel a change in the weather, right there through the telephone, and sure enough when Horace speaks again his voice is cold. "I'll connect you with the complaints department," he says, coldly, and I say, wait, don't, but it's too late, and he does, and then I'm on hold again.

*

1) Unresponsive.

2) Unwilling to engage the community.

3) Dismissive of parents' legitimate concerns and grievances.

Are Emelie's top three failures as Director, according to a complaint someone files anonymously on the Center for Learning and Teaching's website.

*

If I were still a journalist, I would have written a description of the dog park fire.

Not to mention the men fighting next to the electrical wire.

And the woman who reported that one of them said, "Boom!"

*

The pediatrician said that, yup, there was a nasty virus going around.

"But he's a healthy eleven-year-old," the pediatrician assured me. "Healthy eleven-year-olds do just fine with this bad ol' mammajamma."

*

The pediatrician didn't call my son by name. Instead, he called him "Superstar."

"Hang in there, Superstar," he told my son as we left the examining room.

"Dad" was what he called me.

As in, "And you hang in there, too, Dad."

*

Do I wonder what my father would have done, to what lengths he would have gone, if I had died and my name had been misspelled on my death certificate? Well, yeah.

*

"It was just plain wrong that they booted you off Next Door," someone writes on Front Porch, which is another neighborhood online forum, mostly for people who have for one reason or another been booted off Next Door.

*

Once again, I get Emelie's assistant on the phone instead of Emelie herself. Once again, I am told that Emelie is too busy to come to the phone.

"Busy doing what?" I ask Emelie's assistant, who tells me that Emelie is leading a workshop.

I ask her if a workshop is the same thing as a class.

"No," she says. "A workshop is for teachers."

I ask which teachers.

"All of them," she says.

Well, I wonder, if the teachers are in the workshop, then where are the students, and Emelie's assistant says, "Oh, they're in class."

*

My son could be cranky, and contrary. And when I say "could be" I really mean "usually was."

But he was always very sweet when he was sick.

"Thank you so much," he said that night, when Emelie and I brought him a cold washcloth, some aspirin, several comic books, a whole sleeve of saltines.

*

"Sir," a voice says. I look up and there are two cops standing in front of me. One of them is holding a cell phone, and he places it in front of my face. "Sorry to bother you, but we're asking everyone in the neighborhood: Do you recognize this man?"

On the phone is a photo, a photo taken probably by another camera phone and from a great distance. In the photo, there is a man who is looking at his own phone.

"I can't be totally sure," I tell the cops, "but I think it's the man who earlier today was fighting with another man next to a downed electrical wire."

"Thank you," one of the cops says. But then he sees the "go fuck yourself" handwritten on the main office's typed note. "Vandals," he says to the other cop as they start walking away. "I better call the main office and let them know."

*

"I'm not choking myself," my son said, after I told him for Christ's sake to stop choking himself. "I'm *pretending* to choke myself."

*

"Lawyerly," is what my son's sixth-grade teacher called him, when he was still alive.

*

My father had a strong sense of property—odd for someone who stole water. Snowmobilers sometimes cut across our two acres on the way to someone else's two acres and this must have offended my father's sense of boundaries because one late fall he put up fence posts and strung barbed wire, neck high to a man riding a snowmobile. Three weeks later the first snowmobiler of the season almost had his head cut off by my father's barbed wire—although my father argued to the police that since the snowmobiler was trespassing it would be more accurate to say the snowmobiler had almost cut his own head off.

*

4) Requires teachers to take workshops when they should be teaching.
5) Leaves students unattended in their classrooms.
6) Too often relies on clerical staff to be the Center's public-facing representatives.

*

"Good night," I would say to my son, every night, right before he went to sleep.

"Good night," he would say back.

"Have a good sleep."

"Have a good sleep."

"See you tomorrow."

"See you tomorrow."

*

Suddenly I'm no longer on hold. It's like being woken up from a dream in a dream.

"Hello, this is Susan," a voice says on my phone. I assume it's the same Susan, although I can't tell for sure: After all, I only heard her say a few words earlier before she hung up. "So," she says, "you'd like to lodge a complaint against Horace."

"Fuck that guy!" I hear Horace yell in the background, followed by crashing sounds, and then more yelling.

"Actually," I said, "I have no problem with Horace."

"Well, I wish you'd have said that earlier."

"I'm saying it now," I say. "Earlier was only a few minutes ago."

"Earlier would have been in time. Now is too late."

"Someone misspelled my son's name on his death certificate," I say. "That's what I'm complaining about."

"It does happen, and for that we apologize," Susan says, and that's when I know it's the same Susan from before.

"Please don't hang up on me again," I say.

"Oh," Susan says. Her voice is cold now, too. "Would you like me to connect you to the complaints department?"

I don't point out that I thought Horace had already connected me to the complaints department. Because if I do I'm afraid Susan will put me on hold, or hang up on me, and if that happens I'll throw my phone against the wall of the main office—I'm still standing outside the main office—and then I'll keep throwing my phone until I destroy it, and then how will I call the number to get them to spell my son's name correctly on his death certificate?

"No, that's not necessary," I say.

"Well, in that case," Susan says, "let's see how I can help you."

"I would very much appreciate that," I say. That sounds sarcastic but I mean it sincerely. So sincerely that I think I might cry.

Poo-wah poo-wah Siwas.

"Now, what's your name?" Susan asks.

I tell her, spelling it out for her just in case.

"Thank you," Susan says. "Now . . ." But then she stops talking, for one beat, and then another, and then asks, "Wait, is that you standing out there?" Susan wants to know. I look up and see, in a second story window, blinds being separated by fingers, before closing again. "You can't be standing out there."

"Why not?"

"It's considered harassment."

"No, it isn't," I say.

"I bet you were the one who handwrote an obscenity on our note."

I tell her it wasn't me, although that doesn't sound at all convincing, not even to me.

Or, I should say, especially to me. Because I *was* the one, in fact, who wrote "go fuck yourself" on the note.

"You need to leave," Susan says.

"I'm not going anywhere," I say. "I'm not going anywhere until I get what I want."

"See," Susan says. "That's something a harasser would say."

I think about that. Susan's right, of course, and that makes me want to scream at her until my throat bleeds. Which is also of course something a harasser would want to do.

"Go home," Susan says, "and call us back." Then she hangs up.

*

"I'm starting to worry," Emelie said that night. We were standing in the doorway of our son's bedroom. He was in bed, wheezing loudly while watching something on his tablet.

"He's going to be fine," I insisted. "I told you what the pediatrician said."

But it's true that our son looked awful. His face was the color of wet cardboard, even in the flickering light of the screen.

*

One Sign that You're Delaying the Inevitable, is the real title of every list ever written.

*

"You could have really hurt that man," my mother said to my father after the police had left, after they said they wouldn't press charges as long as he took down all the barbed wire.

"He didn't *literally* get his head almost cut off," my father said. "He just got a little scratched up."

"You could have really hurt that man," my mother insisted. "What were you thinking?"

My father didn't say anything. He hung his head, ashamed. Because I bet that what he'd been thinking was that he really wanted to hurt that man.

*

I get another alert on my phone.

This man is a murder suspect, and also a suspect in the Colonial Ponds Dog Park fire. He's considered dangerous. Please, if you see him, keep your distance and call the police.

And then the photo of the man. It's the same photo of the same man the cops showed me. The one who I said might be the man who earlier had been fighting next to the downed electrical wire.

*

At a crosswalk the sign says don't walk, and so I don't walk. I don't walk for some time. Until I realize that no one is walking, and no one is driving. There are only red lights. And then all the lights change at once. They don't go to green. There are, suddenly, no lights at all.

*

Nothing works, nothing works, nothing works. Although surely this is just dumb pessimism, and *something* must work.

*

We were woken the next morning by our son's coughing, which sounded like coins rattling in a pan. His face now was bright red and shining and his skin was hot to the touch.

It was five a.m. The pediatrician's office opened at seven-thirty.

"But there'll be a doctor on call," Emelie pointed out.

I looked at my son, who seemed to have fallen back to sleep. Or maybe he'd never really even woken up, although it was hard to imagine a sleeping person could have coughed liked he'd coughed and stayed asleep.

"He's asleep," I whispered. "We can't even take his temperature without waking him up."

"I guess," Emelie said. When she's nervous, Emelie rubs her fingers together like a mantis. At least, she used to do that. At least, she was doing it then.

"Let's just wait until the office is open," I whispered to Emelie. "We'll call then."

*

What was I waiting for? I don't know what I was waiting for.

*

I continue walking back to my apartment. At the next intersection are two men, two women, wearing bright colored clothing, dancing wildly, badly, and waving to passersby, and to each other. At their feet, a boom box, playing frenetic, upbeat music. Top Forty music, stuff my son would listen to in his room, stuff he'd make us listen to in the car. One of the men is holding a sign. On it, the message EXPERIENCE JOY!!! On the man's face, on all of their faces, is the same avid, intense expression that was on the faces of the two men wrestling over the downed electrical wire, and also the look on my father's face when he'd strung his barbed wire.

*

I didn't do it, says a post on Front Porch, but then that poster doesn't say what it was he didn't do.

*

"Such a sweetheart," is what my son's sixth-grade teacher called him, after he died.

*

The last time I saw my father he was in hospice. It was winter, flu season. Visitors were required to wear surgical masks. My father wasn't wearing a surgical mask, because of course he was in hospice and certain to die, and there was no protecting him. But if there was no protecting him, why was I wearing a surgical mask?

"Take off that stupid thing," my father said, and I did.

I wasn't yet married. My son wasn't born yet. I mention this because if my father had died after I'd been married, after my son was born, those would have been two things we could have talked about.

As it was, we talked about the weather. My father asked what it was like outside, and I told him we were in the middle of a thaw. My father nodded. I wondered if he was thinking what I was thinking: about all those times he dunked himself into that icy hole. How did he bring himself to do it? Did he think that he'd done it once, so he could do it again? Or did he somehow forget how bad it was, so that every time he went into the hole was like the first time he was going into the hole?

"I can't believe how many times you went into the hole," I told him.

My father seemed genuinely confused.

"What hole?" he wanted to know.

*

"The Traditional Media Outlet is short-staffed," my editor tells me on the phone. "How'd you like to dust off your little spiral bound notebook and go cover a fire at the dog park?"

*

Since my son has died, have I thought about killing myself? Of course. All the time. But I'm glad I didn't. Because if I'd killed myself, then how would have I gotten them to spell my son's name correctly on his death certificate?

*

"Thanks, but I can't," I tell my editor. "I'm busy getting them to spell my son's name correctly on his death certificate."

*

I call the main office again and Susan picks up again. I suppose she must recognize my number because she says, without even saying hello, "Sir, are you home now?"

I tell her I am, but I'm not. I'm only halfway there, and in fact am near the dog park fire. I can smell the smoke, can hear the sirens. If I were writing for the Traditional Media Outlet, I would say that even from blocks away you can hear the high, desperate barking of frightened dogs, but truthfully I can't hear any sort of barking at all.

"Good," Susan says. "So, you say your son's name was misspelled."

This makes it sound like Susan, or someone else in the main office, wasn't responsible for the misspelling. That it was someone else's fault. But I'm smart enough by now not to say that. "On his death certificate," I say. "Yes."

"OK," Susan. "Can you tell me how his name was misspelled and how it should be spelled."

I do that. Susan asks me to spell it again, just to be sure, and I spell it again.

"So apparently what we did," Susan says, and it sounds as though she's talking more to herself than to me, or to Horace, if Horace were still in the room, and I assume he has been fired and is not, "was take the 'e' off the end of his last name and put it on the end of his first name."

"It does happen," I say, "and for that you apologized. Which I appreciated," I'm quick to add.

Susan doesn't say anything. Not for one beat, not for several beats. While I'm waiting for her to talk, a woman walks past me. The woman is another person I'm not going to describe, except to say that she has white ear buds sticking out of her ears, and that she looks at me with such intense hatred that I think, for a second, that she's going to strike me, and that I deserve it, even though I'm certain I've never seen her before.

Anyway, I watch the woman walk away from me until she turns a corner, and is out of sight, and then I say to Susan, "Hello?" and she says, "You lied to me."

"I did?"

"You said you were calling me from home," Susan says.

"I am calling you from home," I say.

"Do you live on the street?"

"No," I say, "I live in an apartment."

"Then you're lying when you say you're calling me from home," Susan says. "Because I just walked past you on the street." Then she hangs up.

*

I felt so good, putting my fist through the wall. That sensation of breaking through into a whole other space. But when I tried to extract my fist, it got stuck in the hole, and I had to wiggle it around to get it out, and the drywall crumbled and dropped to the floor and made a mess that I would have to clean up and then I felt so stupid.

*

"It was this guy," says the follow up post on Front Porch.

And then, a photo, again taken from a great distance, of a man, standing next to two cops, looking at a phone. The man, it seems, is me.

*

A week after our son died, I asked Emelie when she wanted to have dinner and she said, "2019."

*

Although back in 2019 my son and I were having an argument. It was about a friend of his who had taken up fencing. I was always haranguing my son to do something interesting. Meaning, to do something that he wasn't doing. Which wasn't much. As far as I was concerned.

"Fencing!" I said, lamely. "Cool!"

"It's not cool," my son said. "It's lame."

"Well," I said, "I think it's pretty cool."

"Well, it's not," my son said.

And so on.

Emelie was in the room, watching this, not saying anything, and so I finally stopped in the middle of the argument and asked if she had anything she wanted to say and she said, "I wish I were somewhere else."

*

At 7:30, our son seemed a little better, or at least hadn't gotten any worse. His temperature was the same. His cough might have sounded a little less painful. He was sitting up, awake, wondering if he could please have some ginger ale.

Maybe, I said, we should give it another hour or so.

Emelie looked at me, nodding, nodding. It was like she was doing some kind of calculation. The past, plus the present, equals what future?

"Fuck that," she finally said. "I'm calling the pediatrician."

Emelie called the pediatrician's office. Our son's pediatrician was on vacation, and so she talked to one of the other pediatricians.

"He called it *what*?" that pediatrician wanted to know.

"'A bad ol' mammajamma,'" Emelie said, repeating what I had said, looking at me while she said it.

"I don't know what that means," said the pediatrician, "but it's a very serious virus."

"How serious?" Emelie wanted to know.

"You probably should have called us earlier," the pediatrician said.

"Well, I'm calling you now," Emelie said.

"*Now*," the pediatrician said, "is when you should be taking your son to the hospital."

*

I notice, as I walk back to my apartment, that every fifth car has one of its doors open and on one of the front seats are the emptied contents of the ashtray, the door's side pocket, the glove compartment. It doesn't look like anything has been stolen. It looks more that the would-be thief was frustrated to discover that there was nothing in any of those cars worth stealing.

*

I know what I was waiting for. I was waiting for my son to get better without us having to call the doctor. And then I would be able to think, and maybe even say, I told you he was going to get better without us having to call the doctor.

*

Emelie calls me. There she is, suddenly, a voice in my ear.

"Did you leave an anonymous complaint about me on the center's website?"

Anger: It starts out righteous, but then where does it go? What happens to it? It turns into shame, and then regret, and then I'm ready to deny everything.

"No, why would I do that?"

"It's in the form of a list."

"Huh," I say. And then, "Hey, I feel like I'm making some headway with the death certificate people."

"And then there was another anonymous complaint," Emelie says. "Also in the form of a list."

Emelie doesn't sound mad. She just sounds tired. Bored. Like there's not one thing I could do to surprise her ever again. No especially ingenious expression of cruelty or kindness. Nothing that could give her pleasure, or pain, or hope. Nothing, except, maybe, some sort of time travel, some magic trick in which I return us to the past or turn the past into the present.

"I'm not making lists anymore," I say. "In fact, I'm just about to write something for the newspaper about the big dog park fire."

*

My son said he had a project for music class. This was a year before he died, when he was ten years old. He wouldn't tell me what the project was, just that he had one.

He then went into the basement, from which emerged, for the next hour, various sounds of struggle and frustration.

Finally, he walked up from the basement, reeking of bleach. In his hand was a white plastic Clorox bottle. My son had emptied the bottle, cut out one of the sides of its belly. On either side of the opening he'd punched holes, and through those holes he'd loosely laced what looked like butcher's string.

He was smiling, hugely. I'd never seen him so happy, so proud. But of course I didn't say that. Instead I said, "Hey, whaddya got there?" and he said, "I made this lute!"

*

"It wasn't me," I post on Front Porch. "I had nothing to do with anything."

"Why should we trust you, Silas?" someone immediately responds and points out that, after all, I'd already proved myself unreliable by getting kicked off Next Door for writing the word "shit" before joining Front Porch.

*

How did this person know my name, I wonder, until I remember that in order to get on Front Porch, I had to register using my name, and also my reasons for wanting to join Front Porch.

*

"You know," I say on my former editor's voicemail, "as it happens I'm near the dog park anyway. Let me take a crack at it."

*

A cell phone number or an email address. That was another thing I had to submit in order to get on Front Porch.

"And now I know who you are, SILAS," reads a text from a number I don't recognize.

I try to get on Front Porch, to see who might have registered using that cell phone number, but it turns out I've been kicked off Front Porch, too.

*

Poo-wah, poo-wah Siwas.

*

"I was just joking!" my son would say, after saying the cruelest, truest thing.

"You look really old," was the last one of those cruel, true things he said to me.

*

"I loved you as a kid, and I love you now, and I guess I'll love you forever," my mother said. This was after my father's funeral. I want to say right after, but it might have been a day, a week, a month. "But no, all you ever think and talk about is your son-of-a-bitching father."

*

My mother died of a heart attack not long after my son was born, and so I can't tell her now that, no, thinking and talking about my father is not all I ever do. For instance, I've been thinking about my son, finally, after all these months. That's been the one good thing to come out of them misspelling his name on his death certificate.

*

"I forgot to ask," I text Emelie on my way to the dog park. "Do you want to have dinner?"

"With you?" she texts back immediately.

And then, three minutes later, she texts, "Let me think about it."

*

"Bob Steve Wagner" is the name of the labradoodle owned by Iris Rexney, 29, who is pulled away from me, and the fire, by Bob Steve Wagner before I can ask her any more questions.

*

I no longer have a car, there being nowhere I especially need or want to go. But the last time I remember driving a car was when Emelie and I rushed our son to the hospital. He was in the backseat lying down with a blanket over him. It was the first time we'd not insisted he put on his seatbelt. I was driving. Emelie was in the front passenger seat. I wasn't looking at her, so I don't know what she was doing. I was looking at the road. It was a road I'd driven on a million times. I was driving on it faster than usual, faster than was legal. It was the middle of the day, but it was foggy, and I couldn't see much, even with my headlights on.

"Be careful!" Emelie shouted.

"I am being careful!" I shouted back, although I wasn't being careful, and in any case Emelie wasn't talking about my driving. Up ahead, the cars were slamming on their brakes, their brake lights looking angry in the gloom. I slammed on my brakes, too, before I could see what was causing any of this. Finally, I did: In the middle of the city, in the middle of a busy street, for no evident reason, there was a sharp dip in the road, and then the pavement turned into rubble. Not gravel, but big sharp rocks, the kind that you can hear threatening the integrity of your tires. The fog was so thick, we couldn't see how long this was going to go on, or why.

"Oh my God," Emelie cried out. "What happened to the road?"

*

I walked past that section of the road earlier. One lane is fixed, and normal. The other lane is still rubble.

*

Oh, by the way, my father took down only some of his barbed wire.

*

"She usually comes right when I call," says Marcus Tinsdale, 52, of Honeybear, a chow mix, who is still in the dog park. Tinsdale calls her name from the sidewalk once, twice, three times, and still Honeybear does not come.

*

"Is it possible that what I hear on Front Porch and Next Door is true? That you were the one who set the dog park on fire?" Emelie texts.

"No," I text her back. "The guy who did it is blaming me. Because I narced on him to the police."

I wait for a response. I wait, and I wait, and then I text, "You don't really think it was me, do you?"

"No," Emelie texts back. "But did you tell me the truth when you said it was not you who complained about me in list form on the center's website?"

"No," I text back.

I wait for a response. I wait, and I wait, and then I text, "But I really am writing a piece for the newspaper about the dog park fire."

Emelie texts back right away. "Why would you lie about THAT?" she wants to know.

*

"What about dinner?" is a follow-up text I manage not to send.

*

There's so much smoke that it's hard to see that there even *is* a dog park. So much smoke that it's hard to see the flames. But I can feel the heat, can hear trees crackling and bursting. Someone inside the smoke yells and then someone else yells back, and then I hear dogs barking and yelping and then I hear nothing but the chunk chunk chunk of something overhead.

I look up and there's a helicopter, hovering over the park. Suspended from the bottom of the helicopter, from cables, is an enormous sagging tarp. The tarp flaps to one side and water dumps out. I didn't know that water could sound like that, like a heavy thing hitting another heavy thing. It's as violent and dangerous seeming as the fire itself. The water makes a hissing sound that drowns out all the other sounds. Steam races up, and the helicopter disappears in it for several seconds before it rises and flies away, the tarp dangling like a broken limb.

*

"Don't you want to know why I did it?" the anonymous texter says. Although of course I know who he is, even if I don't know his name.

"Because he tried to push you onto the wire first," I suggest.

"Obviously. But no, I meant the dog park fire."

"You hate dogs?" I suggest.

"What?" he texts back. "No. God. Who hates dogs?"

*

After my mother said that my father was a son of a bitch, I felt some response was required.

"I loved him," I told her, even though I wasn't sure it was true and I'm still not sure.

"Of course you did," she said, like there was something wrong with my loving him, or my saying I loved him.

"Come on," I said, "he was my *father*."

"Yes," my mother said. "But you know one important thing to remember about your *father*? He was his own worst enemy, while at the same time managing to be other people's worst enemy, too."

*

"Sorry," says the first of three texts from my former editor and current vetter and fact checker. "When you turned it down we assigned the dog park fire story to someone else."

*

"I'll expect your next list on my desk first thing in the morning," says the second text.

*

"Just kidding," says the third text. "Just get the list to me whenever. No hurry at all."

*

"Because," the anonymous texter texts me, "after I'd killed that guy, I wanted to do something like that again. Immediately. And now I still do. So where are you, you big pussy?"

*

This time Susan calls me. I'm not in my apartment. I'm not by the dog park. I have no idea where I am. Probably I've crossed whatever border into another neighborhood, one that has a totally different online neighborhood forum.

"Let's try this again, shall we?" Susan says.

"I'm not at home," I say.

"And I appreciate your honesty," Susan says.

"I'm just sort of wandering around."

"Just clearing your head," Susan suggests.

"It's not working," I tell her.

"It rarely does," she says. "So why don't we focus on your son?"

"You misspelled his name on his death certificate."

"That has been established," Susan says. "But right now, for me, that's all he is. He's just a name, misspelled or otherwise. But here at the main office, we like to get to know the whole person."

I think about that for a moment. It always sounds good, getting to know the whole person. But does it ever happen? Is it possible? And if it is, does it ever end up making anyone happy?

"Would you like me to tell you what he was like?" I ask anyway.

"I think that might be helpful, yes," Susan says.

So I do. I tell her some of the things I've already told you. After I'm done, Susan doesn't say anything. I tense up and realize I'm half expecting her to walk past me again with that look on her face.

Finally, Susan clicks her tongue, disapprovingly. And of course this is what I've been worried about all along. Not that I wouldn't remember my son, but that my remembering wouldn't be good enough.

"Everyone only talks about the good stuff," Susan says. "It's implausible."

"You want to hear about the bad stuff?"

"Yes," Susan says. "And don't tell me there isn't any."

"I won't," I say, and then I do: I tell her all the bad stuff I've told you. Plus, something I just remembered, about the cat, who my son named Butter. We assumed he loved the cat. But our son accidentally let Butter out one day, and the cat was run over by a car and killed right in front of our son's eyes. We tried to console our son, but he resisted our attempts, and in fact didn't seem to need consolation, and in fact didn't seem to feel guilty about letting Butter out the door. Our son had essentially led Butter to her death and yet, he didn't seem to feel anything about that at all.

"Butter was kind of a pain" is how he explained it.

*

When I'm done, I feel sick to my stomach. Like I've eaten too big a meal and want to take it back. Except that's one of the many things you can't take back.

"That was too much," Susan says.

"That was what you asked me," I remind her.

"Just because I asked you for something," Susan says, "doesn't mean you have to give it to me." Then she hangs up.

*

We were in the hospital. Our son was being taken into the ICU. We waved to him, like he was about to go on a cruise. Why did we wave to him? I suppose we didn't know what else to do. He didn't wave back. I could hear him crying and coughing as the orderly wheeled him away. The next time we saw him he had an oxygen mask over his face. The next time we saw him after that he was on a ventilator. The next time we saw him after that he was dead.

But that wouldn't be until three days later. For now, Emelie and I just stood in the emergency room, trying not to look at each other, but also not knowing where else to look.

"Why didn't I call the pediatrician earlier?" Emelie wanted to know. I sensed she was talking to herself, but I answered anyway.

"Because I said we didn't need to."

"But why the hell would I listen to *you*?" Emelie said, raising her voice, and I raised mine to match it.

"Because you wanted me to be right!"

"It was *you* who wanted *you* to be right!" she screamed, right there in the ER, and out of the corner of my eye I watched a security guard stand up out of his rolling chair.

"If that's true," I screamed back, "then why didn't you call the pediatrician earlier?"

*

I wonder if it was the sight of the security guard that made me say something—scream something, actually—that would then so enrage

Emelie that she would punch me in the face, which would then require the intervention of the security guard?

*

Emelie calls me. A good sign. No one ever calls with bad news when they could text with bad news.

"I've thought about it," she says. "And I'm not going to have dinner with you."

"Not tonight or not ever?" I say, fishing. But she doesn't say anything to that. She doesn't say anything and doesn't say anything.

"Why did you call to tell me this instead of texting?" I finally ask her and she says that she didn't want the last thing she ever said to me to be a text.

"Oh," she adds. "And I read the dog park fire story."

"I didn't write it," I say.

"I know," she says.

"But I didn't exactly lie about writing it, either," I say.

"Goodbye, Silas," she says, and then she hangs up.

*

I call the main office and it says its mailbox is full.

*

Will he strangle me? Will he tie a plastic bag around my head and throw me into the river? Will he shoot me, garotte me, hang me, run me over with his car, stab me, dismember me with a chainsaw, find another downed electrical wire and throw me onto it?

"Come and get me," I text the guy, along with my address.

"Hey," the guy texts back, "isn't that near Customs and Alterations?"

*

There's a man leaning against a car parked outside my apartment building, but it isn't the man from the photo, the man who's been texting me, the man who threw the other man onto the live wire. This man looks nothing like that man. This man is much bigger, for instance.

"Silas Bartone?" this man says.

"*What*," I say. Which was another thing my son used to say, when you called his name. Not "yes" but "*what*." Always said in the rudest tone possible.

"I knew it was you because you look pissed off," the man says, also looking pissed off. And sounding pissed off, too.

And that's now how I know who he is: I recognize his voice.

"You're Horace," I say.

"That's right," he says. "The motherfucker you tried to get fired down at the main office."

He moves away from the car, and toward me. Then he grabs me. I mean, he takes a fistful of my shirt, right below the collar. It's the first time anyone has touched me in . . .

Maybe that's why I ask him if he wants to come in.

*

He's the first person to be in the apartment, other than me, since Emelie.

Some things have changed.

There is, of course, the calendar.

I have five pieces of furniture. Six, if you count the toilet.

But still, there's the murmuring of the sewing machines coming from downstairs.

Not to mention the hole Horace doesn't see underneath the calendar.

"This is the loneliest place I've ever seen," Horace says.

Then Horace leaves, without saying anything, without closing the door behind him. I sit down on my couch and close my eyes.

What am I going to do now?

This is the question my therapist has told me to never ask myself.

What's next!

This is the sentence my therapist has told me to say instead. Making sure to use the exclamation point, not the question mark, never the question mark.

What's next is that the guy will show up to murder me, and that will be it. But what if he doesn't? What then?

"Get up!" It's not my therapist who says this. It's Horace.

I open my eyes and Horace is back inside my apartment. In one hand he's holding two slabs of wood with holes in them. In the other hand, is a large mesh bag full of smaller solid bags. Some are red, some are blue.

The slabs of wood have little retractable front legs that, when extended, raise the hole higher than most of the rest of the board. Horace sets one up at the far end of the living room, the other in the kitchen.

"Where did you get all this?" I ask Horace.

"From the trunk of my car," Horace says.

"Why was all this in the trunk of your car?" I ask, and Horace looks at me as though I've asked the dumbest question he's ever heard in his whole entire life.

"It's cornhole," Horace says.

*

Each player gets four bags. Both players stand next to each other and try to throw their bags into the hole. And/or land their bags on the board. And/or knock their opponent's bags off the board.

It's called cornhole because there are those holes in the boards. And presumably the bags are full of corn. They make a peaceful soft rattling sound, almost a *shush* as you toss them from one hand to the other.

We play. One point for each bag that lands on the board. Three for those that go into the hole. Neither of us say anything, except for Horace calling out the score. He is much better than me. I throw my bags too low, not enough arc, and they go skidding off the board. His arc high and land with a good, solid thump on the board, or on the floor when they go through the hole.

Once, because of the thumping, someone from Customs and Alterations bangs on their ceiling. Horace ignores it, and so I ignore it, and we keep ignoring it until it stops happening.

When Horace wins a game he says, "Game." And then, "Again?"

Horace wins the first game twenty-one to five. The second, twenty-one to five. The third, twenty-one to three.

Still, there is something satisfying about the sound of the bags thumping against the boards, or the floor. It's like a tired body falling onto a good mattress.

"Again?" Horace says, and I nod.

Loser goes first. I throw my bag, blue, and it lands on the board and skids, but just a little, a corner of the bag hanging over the hole.

"Nice," Horace says. He tosses his bag, which hits and skids off the board. But before it does, it nudges my bag into the hole. Three points for me, instead of just one.

Horace curses, softly, and then says, "Susan said you went too far."

"I went too far," I admit. "In both directions."

"People always go too far with Susan," Horace says. "She drives them to it. It's part of her character. Yeah, there's no middle ground with Susan."

I take a breath, step, toss. The bag lands again on the board, and sticks, not skidding at all, a hair to the left of the hole.

"Nice," Horace says again.

"Thank you," I say.

"Try again," Horace says.

I look at him. What does he mean, try again? This is the first time I've been ahead. Is this some rule of cornhole that I don't yet know, that when you go ahead for the first time, you get to try again?

But Horace isn't talking about cornhole.

*

My son needed a haircut. I'd been telling him so for months.

"You just *wish* you needed a haircut," my son told me.

If I were still describing things, by the way, I would have already described how bald I am. Very.

"You *really* need a haircut," I insisted, and he just glared at me, through the curtain of hair hanging over his face. He looked like he would have been happy to cut me with his switchblade, if only I'd gotten him a switchblade for his birthday like he'd asked for, *Dad*.

Finally, I prevailed. I don't remember how. By threat, or bargaining, or both. All I remember is that however I prevailed, I felt lousy, diminished, in a kind of permanent way.

"Don't come in with me," my son said, outside the barbershop, not looking at me, staring straight ahead through his hair. "Just give me the money."

He stuck out his hand. I did what I was told. Then I sat in the car. What were my thoughts? I did not have any thoughts. I was trying not to have any thoughts. I was afraid of them, and of him, and myself.

But then a half hour later, he came out of the barber shop, unwrapping his sucker. I could see his face. I could even see some of his forehead. He waved at me, and smiled. And there he was. My beautiful baby boy.

*

"Game," Horace says. I'd like to say I win. But no, it's him again. Twenty-one to nine.

"Again?" I ask

"I can't," he says. "Gotta get back to work."

"Of course," I say. We shake hands. Then Horace packs up his cornhole set and leaves. But even though he's gone, the apartment seems like a brighter, more lived-in place. I sit down on the couch, and suddenly I can see the future. In it, Horace will be back, and we'll play some more cornhole, and maybe I'll get better at it, maybe over time I'll even be able to give him a run for his money, and when Horace is not at the apartment playing cornhole I'll be calling him and Susan at the main office from right here on my couch in my quest to get my son's name spelled correctly on his death certificate. And this will be a thing that will go continue to go on and on.

*

Six Backyard Games That Will Change Your Life will be my next list, if I can figure out what the other five games might be.

*

Oh, and I get a notification on my phone. Suspect is in custody. The dog park fire is under control. Expect no further alerts.

*

But a minute later Horace is back. There's a sheepish look on his face. An envelope in his hand. "Don't tell the main office I almost forgot to give you this." He hands me the envelope and leaves again.

I open the envelope. Inside is a new death certificate. On it, my son's name, his first and middle and last, all spelled correctly. Nothing left to complain about. No one to call and no reason to call them. It's all over. He's really dead. And only then do I realize what I've done.

MEMPHIS

I drove into Memphis, stopped at the first bar I saw inside the city limits, and while drinking my drink I overheard a man telling the story of how his brother had killed a man by biting off his hard cock. I immediately took out my phone, logged into my blog, a blog you might not have heard of, a blog called An Expert on Cities I Just Got To, and was about to write, "Memphis is a city where men murder other men by biting off their hard cocks," but then I stopped, and grew thoughtful. Because there, on my phone, scrolling back in time and space, was the entirety of the human story, or at least the entirety of my human story, or at least the entirety of the last six months of my human story, told in one-sentence expert summations of cities I'd just got to, starting with Fresno, which is a city where men do not murder other men by biting off their hard cocks but rather a city where women murder other women by running each other over with their F-150s in convenience store parking lots; and then Sacramento, which does not proofread its billboards; and Santa Fe, which is always just sold out of dream catchers; and Denver, which smells of dog food; and Oklahoma City, where gas isn't nearly as cheap as it is in Tulsa; and Seattle, where people put bumper stickers on their bicycles; and Billings, where everyone has conjunctivitis; and Indianapolis, where children look like future librarians; and Columbus, where every adult walks around with some kind of gross glistening orange shit smeared all over their face; and Cincinnati, where every adult walks around smoking candy cigarettes; and Boston, where white women ask each other how anyone could think they were racist; and Tampa, where black men in juice bars loudly sing along to the song "Mr. Jones" by the Counting Crows when it comes on the radio; and Lubbock, where people exclusively drink soft drinks the color of urine; and so on. One hundred and ninety-nine cities visited, briefly, and then blogged about, briefly, and Memphis would be my two hundredth. A milestone. An occasion worth noting, and celebrating. Although it's difficult to celebrate when you're by yourself, and the bar I was in was mostly empty, and I didn't think the man whose brother had killed another man by biting off his hard cock would want to celebrate with me, especially after I explained to him what we were celebrating. So I called my father.

"Where are you?" my father said, because if my father were a city, he'd be a city where people don't say hello when answering the telephone.

"Memphis," I told him. "It's my two-hundredth city, it'll be my two-hundredth post!" I explained what I was about to write about Memphis in my blog, and then waited to hear him say wow, congratulations, well done, something like that. Instead, for a while, all I could hear was his labored breathing. I could picture him. It was after dinner, and he'd be in his kitchen, at the table, drinking a cup of instant coffee and smoking a cigarette, which was why his breathing was so labored. We—my two brothers and my sister and I—had been on his case to quit smoking, but he wouldn't, I think because it reminded him of his wife, my mother, with whom he'd drunk instant coffee and smoked cigarettes every night after dinner, for all twenty-six years of their marriage, until she'd died of lung cancer a couple of years earlier, and I was sure he would die of lung cancer, too, we all were sure of this, even my father himself was probably sure of it, and maybe he wanted it, too, maybe he wanted to die, for reasons he couldn't or wouldn't articulate, not even to himself. Talk to me, Dad, is what I wanted to say, but before I could say that, he said, "I have family in Memphis."

"You do?" I said, and my father said that, yes, he had aunts and uncles and cousins, and the cousins had kids, too, and so he also had whatever you call the children of cousins, they were all related to him, they were all his people, and they all lived in Memphis, and how were they not supposed to think that what I was about to write about Memphis was not something I was saying something directly about them, to them, and how did I think this reflected on him, and I said that I was sorry, that I didn't know he had relatives in Memphis, but even if I had, and even now that I did, I was still going to post it on my blog, and my father said that it would hurt their feelings, and I said that sometimes the truth hurts, and my father said that what I'd written wasn't the truth, it was my snap judgment, my impression of Memphis made after being there for only a minute, and I said, that, yeah that's what I do, I stay in a city for a minute and then make a grand statement about what it means to be from that city, and then my father suggested that I stay in a city for at least a day, a week, a month, before I wrote something about it, and I reminded my dad that we'd been over this already, and my father said that maybe we should go over it again, and so, going over it again, I reminded my father that other people already did what he said I should do in *their* blogs, and that I wanted to do something else, something different, in mine, and then my father suggested that I do something completely different and not write a blog at all, and I said, *Dad*, and then my father said, But you could do lots of things, you were a Communications major, and I said, Oh my God, and my father said, Fine, your brother wants to talk to you.

Because I'd forgotten: It was Sunday. And every Sunday my brothers and my sister and their families came over to my father's house for dinner.

"Hey, guy," my oldest brother said, because if he were a city, he would be a city in which people call other people "guy" even if the other person wasn't a guy. "What's Dad so riled up about?"

I told him. My brother, who works in conflict resolution in his company's human resources office, listened, without interrupting. I could picture him, leaning against the counter, nodding thoughtfully as he listened, and when I was done talking, he said, "Well, maybe you could just say it was another city," and I told him, No, that when I'd begun this project, this journey, I'd decided that I would never change the name of the city, no matter how unflattering my summation of the city was, I would call it in my blog what it was called in the world, and as I explained all that to my oldest brother, he listened, thoughtfully and then he said, "Well, does the cock have to be hard? Could it be semihard? Could it be soft, or flaccid? And maybe it doesn't have to be a cock. Does it have to be a cock? Could it be a dick, or even a rod? How about a penis? A penis seems like it could work. A penis seems like a compromise everyone could live with. Just think about it. I wish you'd come home, guy. OK, here's Catherine."

"Hi, Meat Pie," my sister said, because if my sister were a city, then she'd be a city in which people never stop referring to their siblings by their childhood nicknames. "What's the story?"

So I told her. I told her about Memphis being a milestone, and what I was going to write about it in my blog, and while I was talking I could hear my sister tapping something with her pencil. Because my sister was a master carpenter, and she was never without a pencil, and a tape measure, and in her truck there were always blueprints, and power tools, the most up-to-date kind, and also lots of antique tools that she insisted that, in the right hands (and hers were the right hands), were in some ways capable of better carpentry than even the most up-to-date power tools, and in this way not only was my sister a master carpenter but she was also a historian of carpentry, and she was good at both jobs, so good that she now had employees, and when I was done telling her about Memphis she said, "You know, I have a story you should write instead of your blog. There's this guy who works for me. Pious Ali. A Somali immigrant, a refugee, he was a doctor in Somalia, but when he had to leave Somalia—and oh man, did he have to leave Somalia, it's a harrowing story, a terrific story, you should get him to tell it to you, you should write it down—he couldn't be a doctor anymore, and so now he works for me. His English is not the greatest, but he's very good with the carved bone awl, nineteenth century, Welsh, you know the awl, very tricky, but Pious is a natural. It's a terrific story, very powerful, very important. You should come home and write it. All right, here's Terry."

"I see you don't have any comments yet," my middle brother said. Because if my middle brother were a city, then he would be a city in which people don't talk, at all, except to remind their siblings of what they don't have. And it was true: I'd blogged about one hundred and ninety-nine cities over the previous six months, and not once had anyone written in the comments section in my blog; not once had a person complained or complimented or corrected something I'd written about their city. I don't know what I'd expected to come out of the blog, but I hadn't expected nothing. But there had been nothing; no one had commented. My middle brother was absolutely right about that. He must have been talking to me from my father's back deck, which overlooked my father's backyard, because I could hear the shouting and laughter of children playing, the shouting and laughter of my nieces and nephews, my middle brother's children and my sister's children and my oldest brother's children, and the sound of them made me feel so lonely, as lonely as I felt whenever I looked at, or thought about, the empty comments section in my blog, although maybe not quite as lonely as I'd felt when I used to go to my father's house every Sunday night, to have dinner with my family, and felt the loneliest I've ever felt, because I knew that was the opposite of what I was supposed to feel. "You should come home," my middle brother said. "Here's Dad again."

"You really should come home," my father said, suddenly, in my ear, and I had the feeling that he'd been listening in on the other line, that he'd been there the entire time.

"I can't," I said, and my father sighed and that sigh turned into a wheeze and then into a cough, and then into a series of coughs, and I had the terrible thought that I'd never see him alive again, and it turns out that I never did.

"What do you want?" my father asked, softly, and I really do think that he wanted to know.

"I want to feel that I belong somewhere in this world, or I want to die," is what I wanted to say, but I didn't know how to say that to my father, or to anyone else for that matter. And so I said, "I just want to keep doing what I'm doing."

"OK, then," my father said, and then he said goodbye and I said goodbye, and then we hung up, and then I wrote, "Memphis is a city where men murder other men by biting off their hard cocks," and then I hit Post, and then I waited to see what would happen next.

ACKNOWLEDGMENTS

Thanks to:

Lawrence Welk for the bubbles, and for his *Wunnerful, Wunnerful! The Autobiography of Lawrence Welk*,

my friend and editor, Nicola Mason,

the magazine editors who originally published these stories: Michael Griffith, Jodee Stanley, Anna Lena Phillips Bell, Ladette Randolph, Adam Ross, Kelly Abbott, and Evgeniya Dame,

my family,

these people, whose ideas, edits, encouragement, and mockery kept me going: Jennifer Brice, Michael Griffith (again), Cassie Jones, Ann Kibbie, Keith Morris, Kevin Moffett, Jason Ockert, Trent Stewart, Corinna Vallianatos, Mark Wethli, and Caki Wilkinson.

The stories in this collection previously appeared in the following publications:

"Special Election," *Ecotone*
"Reckonings," *Joyland*
"Big Velcro," *The Cincinnati Review*

"The Big Book of Useless Saturdays," *The Sewanee Review*
"Chest Bump," *A Very Angry Baby* anthology (Acre Books)
"The Slim Jim," *Great Jones Street*
"One Goes Where One Is Needed," *Ploughshares*
"Customs and Alterations," *The Cincinnati Review*
"Memphis," *Ninth Letter*